A
LANCASTER
STORY

JOY

C.S. POE

Joy

Published by Emporium Press
https://www.cspoe.com
contact@cspoe.com

Cover Art by Reese Dante
Cover content is for illustrative purposes only and any person depicted on the cover is a model.

Edited by Tricia Kristufek
Copyedited by Andrea Zimmerman
Proofread by Lyrical Lines

Published 2020.
First Edition published 2017. Second Edition 2020.
Printed in the United States of America

Digital eBook ISBN: 978-1-952133-14-5
Trade Paperback ISBN: 978-1-952133-53-4

For Mom.
Thank you for teaching me to find joy in everything.

AUTHOR'S NOTE

While each book in A Lancaster Story can be read as a standalone, occasional crossover of characters does occur. Check out each title in the series to fully enjoy all of the residents of Lancaster, New Hampshire.

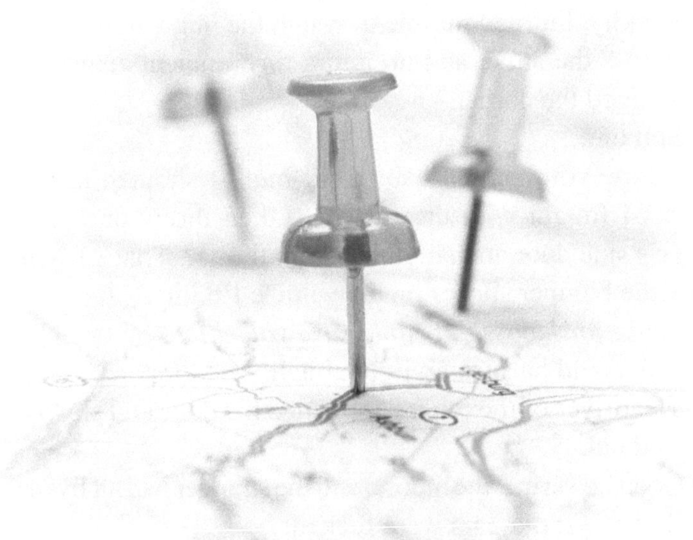

CHAPTER ONE

The first and only thing I've learned about moose was that there was no right way to hit one.

"*Holy shit*," I cried as the animal leaped out from the forest when I rounded a sharp turn of the road. I slammed on the brakes, but my worthless piece-of-crap car skidded into the animal, clipped it, and spun out hard.

I didn't see the car coming from the opposite direction until I hit it, successfully ending my junker's ballerina spins. My seat belt caught me before I went through the windshield, snapping me back against the seat. That hurt. My entire body vibrated with adrenaline as everything came to an abrupt stop.

Steam hissed from under the hood of my car.

Shakily, I turned in time to watch the huge, ugly beast trot across the street and up into a tiny, ancient cemetery that hugged the corner.

Son of a....

"Hope you name a baby after me!" I shouted at the moose. I fought with the seat belt, then threw open the driver's side door and stumbled from the car. That's when I saw the bumper sticker on the vehicle I'd hit.

Brake for moose—It could save your life!

Life could be such an ironic bitch.

The driver of the other car opened his door and slowly climbed out.

Good news: me, the moose, and the stranger had all lived.

Bad news: our cars were fucked.

"Hey," I said, my voice a little wobbly. "Are you all right? It—the moose—it jumped in front of me."

The man removed his worn, frayed cap and scratched his forehead as he studied the damage to his rear end. He was tall. Big—like a mountain. He had a rough-and-tumble country-boy sort of look. His dark hair could benefit from a comb, though, and he desperately needed a shave. The cargo pants and faded flannel over a black T-shirt didn't help turn him around much either.

And he still hadn't spoken.

So I tried again. "You okay?"

The stranger finally nodded and put his cap back on. "Moose do that."

"What? Purposefully try to fuck shit up?"

He stared at me. "You have insurance?"

Fuck. Me. Sideways.

If this impromptu road trip of mine could get any worse, I might as well lie down on the double line and give up now.

But this is my sort of tragic existence. I was Gideon Joy, the most unlucky man this side of the Rockies.

And yes, I realized that was pretty melodramatic. The fact that I had air in my lungs and clothes on my back already put me in a better spot than some. But standing on the side of the road, screwed seven ways to Sunday because of a moose with no manners, I really was feeling the twenty-five years of life's jokes weighing down on my shoulders.

Nothing ever worked out.

Nowhere was ever home.

No one wanted to love a guy with luck so bad, it was laughable.

Now this dude wanted my insurance information, and *fuck* if I had money for that. The state of my car should have said how well I was doing lately. I had no plans to stay in New Hampshire. (Just driving through, thank you very much.) I had only stopped long enough to piss at a rest area and buy vending machine food, because that was the kind of budget I rolled with, and I wasn't looking to delay my trip longer than that.

I had squirreled away enough cash to get me from Los Angeles to Portland, Maine, with hopefully something left over to get me back. I was sightseeing, I guess. Road-trip therapy was more likely. I don't know. It was a rather unplanned excursion.

I ran a hand through my hair and then pushed up my glasses. "I don't, ah, have insurance."

The other man didn't respond, only looked at his car again and rubbed his bristled jaw.

"Do you?" I dared to ask.

Still no answer.

"Hey," I prompted.

"It doesn't cover noninsured motorists."

"Great," I muttered.

I could—well, not get in my car and drive away, because that piece of shit wasn't moving anytime soon. But I could run. He didn't know my name. I wasn't from here. I could just turn around and hitchhike home. Let the dude worry about repairing his own car.

Except that was probably the lowest, most dishonorable action I could take. I didn't have much going for me, but I clung to my pride like a raft adrift at sea. I couldn't walk away from this mess and leave the poor bastard in a predicament as bad as mine.

I glanced up to see him now staring at me. "I'm sorry. I'll get this fixed. I don't know how, because I have no money, but I won't leave you all jacked-up like this."

"Good intentions won't pay for a repair."

"I'm trying to do the right thing," I retorted. "Cut me some slack, will you?"

"I didn't wreck your car," he said, calm as you please.

I relaxed my balled-up hands and took a really deep breath. "*Guy*—"

"Silas."

"What?"

He pointed to himself. "Silas."

Wow. *Silas*? Who the fuck named their kid Silas these days?

He stared at me.

"Silas," I corrected. "Give me a minute to figure this out."

(As if a minute would make me less fucked than I was thirty seconds ago.)

I put my hands on my hips and turned away.

It was quiet. Really quiet.

I hadn't gotten out of my car since becoming lost in the countryside, away from the highways and rest stops. But sure enough, up here in northern New Hampshire, even in the late afternoon—*silence*. There was a brisk breeze blowing, rustling the spring leaves like they were Mother Nature's personal wind chime. It was kind of nice, but a little weird too.

I mean, where were the people? The cars? The sounds of civilization? I'd driven by more animal crossing signs than traffic lights in the last hour.

I turned to Silas. "Where the hell am I, anyway?"

He raised an eyebrow. "In between Lancaster and Dalton."

"Are those the closest cities?"

Silas didn't smile, but I got the distinct impression that the question amused him nonetheless. "Not much in terms of cities in Coös County."

"What does that mean?"

He shrugged and slid his hands into his pockets. "'Bout nine hundred folks in Dalton."

Was he joking?

He was joking.

Right?

Silas didn't say anything else.

"Fuck," I growled. "Look, I'm going to pay for your repairs. It's not like I can skip out on it. Look at *my* car. Do you know if—if any of these nine hundred people are hiring?" I asked, noting the desperation in my tone.

"A bit far from home," Silas said instead.

"What?"

He tilted his chin at my car.

I looked to see he was referring to the California license plate. California wasn't home, though. It was just a place.

"Are there any hotels?" I tried.

Silas eyed me a moment longer before he turned and walked to his car. He paused at the door and made a come-hither motion.

"But what about…?" I jutted a thumb at my car.

"It's not going anywhere."

"Someone might steal it."

Silas had the common courtesy to not respond to that.

Reluctantly, I grabbed my duffel bag from the back seat, locked the doors, and left my car on the side of the road. "Is yours safe to drive?"

"It'll make it to Lancaster," Silas answered.

"Where exactly are we going?"

He didn't respond, merely slid in behind the wheel and shut the door.

Jesus. Awkward, much?

I walked to the passenger side and opened the door. I hesitated for a beat, but really, Silas didn't act like a serial killer or some shit. He was more preoccupied with getting money for repairs than seemingly trying to kidnap me. And I *did* have my cell phone, just in case—if it even got a signal out here….

"Where are we going?" I asked again.

Silas started the car and glanced sideways. "I'll drive you to a place to stay."

"Really?"

"Yes."

I let out a breath and got in.

"I'll see you get my repair bill."

Ass.

"Thanks," I said woodenly.

He pulled onto the road.

"My name's Gideon Joy, by the way."

Silas didn't answer.

"It's nice to meet you," I offered.

More freaking silence.

I turned to stare out the window and caught my reflection in the side mirror. Blond hair combed to one side, scruffy facial hair, glasses, tattoos—*that* must have been the reason behind the silent treatment. I had a lot of tattoos. Maybe too many. They bothered some people. Not that Silas could even *see* most of them, but I did have a large tattoo on my neck, as well as on either hand. One or two tended to be okay with the general population, but once you were as colorful as a canvas, I'd noticed people were more than happy to share their opinion of how I'd regret my decisions or why they made me unattractive.

So maybe in this backwater craphole, looking different was bad. Or maybe Silas simply thought my artwork was ugly. Not that I cared, because he wasn't winning any beauty contests either.... *The jerk.*

Silas parked outside of a big Queen Anne house painted in bright funky shades of blue, green, and pink. He turned the car off and climbed out, which I assumed was my indication to follow. There was a sign beside the front walkway.

Bridget & Bernard's.

"This doesn't look like a hotel," I said, following behind Silas.

"This is cheaper."

"What is it?"

"B&B."

Ah. Bridget & Bernard. B&B. *Funny.*

Silas stopped at the front steps and moved aside to allow me access.

I walked across the porch and knocked loudly on the front door. A little lady opened it. She was older, maybe in her sixties, and came up to about my shoulders, with dyed purple hair and copious amounts of cheap costume jewelry.

Bridget, I presumed.

"Why, hello there," she said cheerfully. "How can I help you?"

"Hey. I'm, uh, looking for a place to stay. I hit a moose—"

"*Oh no*! That's the third accident this week. I swear, those gosh darn beasts…. You okay, honey? You don't need a doctor, do you?"

"No, I'm fine. I just—I also hit his car," I continued, turning to motion at Silas, who was still standing at the base of the porch steps.

Bridget glanced around me and her face lit up. "Silas. How're you doing, sweetie pie?"

"Fine, ma'am."

"*Ma'am*. He always ma'ams me," she said with a chuckle. "If Silas brought you here, don't worry. We'll take good care of you." Bridget patted my arm.

"I might have to stay for a while," I continued at length. "I don't have enough on me to pay for the repairs, so I was going to see about a job in town."

"Look at you—bright young thing, taking responsibility."

I wasn't sixteen. Slow your roll, Bridget.

An older man joined Bridget at the door just then. He was very tall and equally as thin, with spectacles and a pipe. An actual pipe, like ye olden times. These two made for a hell of a pair.

"Who do we have here?" he asked.

"Gideon Joy," I said, shifting my bag to shake his hand.

"Nice to meet you. I'm Bernard Bartholomew, the other half of Bridget and Bernard, as you might well have imagined."

"I did imagine."

"He's needing extended accommodations," Bridget explained, looking up at Bernard. "Poor boy hit a moose *and* Silas's car. You're not from around here, are you?" she asked next, turning to me again.

"Er—no."

"Tourists don't expect the moose and deer. They don't know how to drive around here," she whispered. "No offense."

"None taken, I think," I replied.

"We can probably manage something long-term," Bernard said, puffing thoughtfully on his pipe. The smoke had a heady cherry fragrance that brought with it a sensation of nostalgia. That was decidedly strange, because I was pretty sure I'd never smelled pipe tobacco before.

Bridget stepped out of the doorway, nudged me aside, and walked across the porch. "We'll take care of your Mr. Joy, Silas."

"I'm not his—" I started.

"Need me to call a tow truck for your car?" Bridget continued, speaking over me like she hadn't even heard my attempted protest.

"No, ma'am," Silas answered. "It'll make it to the shop." He nodded politely and made his way back down the walk to his car.

"He's such a good boy," Bridget said. She turned, grabbed my elbow, and hauled me into the house. "There couldn't have been a better car on the road to hit."

Bernard followed us, went to stand behind a counter in the foyer of the huge Victorian home, and flipped through an oversized ledger. More smoke settled around him, like a chimney working overtime. "How long do you think you'll be staying, Mr. Joy?"

"Gideon," I insisted. "And I'm not sure. How far is town from here?"

Bernard looked up with a bemused expression. "This *is* town. Main Street is about a five-minute walk thaddaway," he said, jutting his thumb to the right.

Oh God.

I swallowed. "Well, if there are any jobs available, I'm staying for however long it takes to pay for two car repairs and my time here."

Bridget sidled up beside her husband and hummed thoughtfully. "Babycakes, you're probably looking at a good month. But we can give you a discount for staying on that long."

"That's really nice. Thanks."

"You can stay in the Princess Suite," Bernard declared.

Christ.

So… the Princess Suite was pink.

Really fucking pink.

From the wallpaper to the rugs to the comforter—a sea of pink and frilly lace for as far as the eye could see. But the room was nice. Spacious, clean, and with big windows boasting a gorgeous view of an early sunset. A breeze stirred the gauzy curtains as I leaned closer to the screen for a look at Main Street.

Even with cars more frequent here than on that empty stretch of road where I'd met My Friend, the Moose, and with the echo of voices coming from the yards of nearby homes likely as old as this one, it was still unreasonably quiet. Quaint and quiet and cozy and... *quiet*.

Shit. For the first time since I'd left LA over two weeks ago, I felt like I could take a breath and not choke on uncertainty and self-loathing. I mean, I wasn't okay. That hard knot in my gut was still there, still an ever-present reminder that I was nothing but a fuckup, but at least I didn't feel like throwing up. Until I ruminated on those car repair bills in my immediate future... but one step at a time.

I set my duffel on the foot of the bed and walked out of the suite. There were six rentable rooms in the house, split evenly between the second and third floors, with shared bathrooms for guests. I stood still outside my door and took a brief listen to the sounds of the house, confirming there must have been several guests already occupying the other rooms. I walked to the end of the hall to the bathroom, happy to find it unlocked and empty.

I slipped inside, moved to the mirror over the sink, and frowned at my reflection. I wet my fingers and dragged them through my hair a few times, then adjusted the collar of my button-down shirt. A tie would have made my sorry ass look more professional when I went begging for a job, but of course I didn't have one on me. Actually, I probably hadn't owned a tie since graduating high school. I tugged on the sleeves of my black sweater and tried to brush away the wrinkles before pausing to study the tats on my hands. Fuck all I could do about those, though.

I walked out of the bathroom and down the long hallway, the antique floor creaking underfoot. I went downstairs, crossed the foyer, and exited. Bridget and Bernard were standing in front of the house, both wearing ridiculous matching sunhats and discussing a pile of flowers that looked to have been recently purchased from a garden center.

"How's the room?" Bridget called when I stepped onto the porch.

"Great," I replied. *But I'll never be able to look at pink again after this.*

"Off to job hunt, then?" Bernard asked next.

I nodded and walked down the porch steps. "Any advice on where to go?"

The Bartholomews looked at each other.

"Or… what to avoid?" I finished awkwardly.

"You should stay away from Bucker's," Bridget answered.

"What's Bucker's?"

"A bar."

I perked up a bit. "I know how to bartend, though."

Bridget made a face. "The owner isn't…. That is… there are more accepting folks in town to work for."

"He doesn't like *flatlanders*," Bernard supplied.

"Or gays," Bridget added in a loud whisper.

"Honey," Bernard murmured.

"What?" she protested. "He doesn't."

I cleared my throat.

Bridget smiled, came forward, and grabbed my hand. "Just because we're a small town in the country doesn't mean we're all closed-minded like that prick."

I held back a laugh at hearing a grandma say *prick*.

"Was it presumptuous of me to say something?" Bridget asked, letting go of my hand.

"Well—no, I mean, you're right." I might have been unsure of most everything in life, but my sexuality was at least one aspect that had its feet firmly planted on the ground.

"Try some of the restaurants," Bernard stated. "Tourists are starting to roll in with the spring weather. Someone is bound to be looking for seasonal help."

"I'll do that. Thank you." I said goodbye and headed off in the direction Bernard pointed me.

The sky was bright pinks and oranges as I reached Main Street. The two-lane road went down for some ways before disappearing around a bend shaded by massive birch and pine trees. There were a few cars coming and going, but I was from LA—I wouldn't call this traffic, let alone rush hour. In the immediate vicinity were a bunch of mom-and-pop shops. There was an antique store, a bank, a clothing store—a *one-room* movie theater?

What hell.

I walked down the sidewalk until I stood in front of a brightly lit window that read Eatery. I shrugged to myself, opened the door, and stepped inside. I wasn't certain what I'd been expecting from a locally owned restaurant way out here in the boonies—something cheap, maybe? Something akin to grandma's kitchen? I don't know, but I felt like a shit for it, because Eatery was actually kinda nice inside.

The wall opposite the bay windows on either side of the front door was decorated in gorgeous stills of what seemed to be the surrounding woodland during the four seasons. The interior was subdued, with fairy lights strung near the ceiling, and each of the tabletops had a lit candle—tiny flames flickering like an actual fairy come to life. The counter had a register and a few stools where regular-looking folks sat.

A pretty woman, younger than me maybe, with purple lipstick and glitter eyeshadow approached, grabbed a menu from a stand beside the door, and said, "Hello there. Table for one?"

I tugged nervously on the cuffs of my shirt. "Actually, I was hoping to speak with the owner. Is… that you?"

She seemed amused by that question and smirked. "Nope, but why don't you take a seat at the counter and I'll go get him."

I thanked her, made my way across the room, and took a seat at an empty stool. I watched the waitress quickly move through a swinging door to the right of the counter, the sounds of a busy kitchen drifting out in her wake.

After a few minutes, a burly guy with dark hair wandered out, and I had to briefly wonder if men only came in extra-extra-large this far north. (Not that I was entirely complaining, mind you.) He zeroed in on me without a flicker of doubt, approached the counter, and while wiping his hands clean on his apron, asked, "Looking for me?"

I stood. "Yes, sir, I think so."

"George Bright," he said, holding a hand out.

I shook his bear paw and tried not to wince. "Gideon Joy."

"How can I be of service, Gideon?"

"I came to—well—inquire as to whether you're hiring. I realize me just walking in off the street isn't that professional…."

George crossed his big arms. "Not a local boy, are you?"

"No."

He nodded minutely. "Figured as much. Folks strolling in off the street, asking about work—it's not unusual in these parts."

"Oh."

"Where you from?"

"California. Los Angeles."

George whistled lightly. "You're awfully far from home Mr. Gideon Joy."

"I was heading to Maine, but I hit a godda—I hit a moose. Now I have repair bills to pay for, and I don't have that kind of cash on me."

"So *you're* the guy who hit Silas's car."

I made a face. "Jesus. Word gets out fast. You guys have signal lights on rooftops or something?"

George snickered. Despite the whites he wore, he didn't look like a chef. He looked like an outdoor survivalist. Bear Grylls, eat your heart out. "Not many young guys in Lancaster lookin' like you."

I instinctively put a hand to my neck, like maybe he wouldn't notice the massive colorful tattoo high above my shirt collar.

But George just smiled. "So you're staying in town for a while?"

"I'm staying at the B&B." I looked over my shoulder, gathered my bearings for a second, then pointed in the direction I'd come from.

"Ah, with the Bartholomews," he answered.

"That's right."

"But you don't have a job to get back to in LA?"

I shifted. "Not… exactly. I quit my job."

George was doing that little head nod again. "Got any restaurant experience?"

I perked up. "Sure."

George looked me over and then narrowed his eyes. "But you crashed your car."

"I'm a good driver," I insisted. "The moose had no chill."

He laughed. "I believe you. They're dumb as hell. Now look—I *do* need some help around here. My 'everything' guy left last week for basic training, and with this nice weather, the construction crews are back to work. They order takeout like their lives depend on it, and I've been scrambling to keep up."

Was this guy going to hire me on the spot?

No résumé?

No references?

No *nothing*?

Who on God's green earth conducted business like this?

"You okay with doing deliveries?" George continued.

I blinked a few times before blurting out, "Y-yes. Of course."

"Dishes too? It's nothing glamorous," he warned.

"I'm totally, perfectly okay with that."

CHAPTER TWO

"Gideon."

I turned with my bin of dirty dishes collected from the dining tables. It was my second day in New Hampshire and my first as the do-what-needs-to-be-done boy at Eatery.

Nancy Sheppard, the purple-lipstick waitress from last night, stood in the open doorway of the kitchen. "You've got your first delivery."

"Sure thing." I walked into the kitchen, set the bin down to wash the contents later, and walked across the hot room.

George glanced up at my approach. He was putting take-out containers in a paper bag. "How's it going so far?"

"Fine," I said.

The routine at Eatery was proving easy enough. Repetitive, messy, sweaty, kind of boring—but I was earning cash I desperately needed, so he had no complaints from me.

"I've got a lunch order that needs to go out," George continued. He shoved the big bag my way and offered the address scribbled on a spare ticket.

I looked at it and stated, "The Bridge."

"Yup." George moved away, already starting to cook his next order.

The fuck did the Bridge mean?

But I didn't want to seem incompetent in front of the guy signing my checks, so I turned, headed out the swinging door again, and called to Nancy as she left a table after filling the water glasses for two customers. "Hey. Nancy. What's this mean?" I held out the ticket with my free hand.

She stopped moving long enough to decipher the chicken scratch. "That's the crew repairing the covered bridge. They order lunch every day."

"Yeah, but am I supposed to type 'Bridge' into the GPS and hope for the best?"

"No, smartass." She chuckled before giving my arm a friendly punch. "Have you been to Dalton yet?"

"Sort of. I met a moose out that way."

"Well, there's only one road, so don't worry about it. You head out of Lancaster," she said, indicating over her shoulder, "past the B&B, yeah? Keep driving for about fifteen minutes, and eventually you'll come to a fork. Left is Dalton, straight ahead is a covered bridge going into Vermont. The crew has been out there for about a week. Around here, we have to hire specialized repairmen because the historical bridges require very specific care."

"Are there street signs to watch out for or—?"

Nancy turned and looked at a local who'd begun laughing from his seat at the counter. "He's not from around here," she explained before turning to me again. "No, honey, just drive. The road will bring you right through into the next town."

She might as well have said, *Take a left at the big oak tree.*

I mean seriously… *just drive*?

But I didn't argue, murmured a thanks and left with the order. Eatery had its own delivery car, which was great for me, considering the current situation. I got in, turned on the radio, and drove in the direction Nancy had explained. Luckily, I was vaguely familiar with this section of Lancaster, and as I approached the B&B, I noticed my junker was parked in the driveway. I slowed down and lowered the volume on a John Deere commercial.

"Yoo-hoo!" Bridget called from the front yard. She waved her garden glove at me, hurried toward the road, and crossed it as I rolled the window down. "George already has you running errands, does he?"

"I'm off to find a bridge," I answered.

"Oh. Keep driving this way for about fifteen minutes," she said, not missing a beat and clearly understanding which specific bridge I was on the hunt for.

"Will do, thanks. Uh, why is my car here?"

Bridget looked back and then said, "Tow truck dropped it off. You didn't want it left on the side of the road, did you?"

"But who paid to have it towed?"

"Silas," she said, as if I should have known.

"The guy I hit," I clarified, deadpan.

Bridget nodded. "Of course."

"Why?"

"Why what?"

"Why did he have my car towed?"

"Because he's a good boy. Anyway, I won't keep you. Drive safe." Bridget put her gloves on and hurried back to her gardening.

I did find the Bridge.

Believe it or not, I just drove *thaddaway* for a few miles and actually came upon a construction crew seemingly in the middle of nowhere. But during the drive there, I tried to figure out why Silas would pay to have my car brought into town. That wasn't exactly cheap. Was he going to give me the bill for that too? I didn't ask him to have the car towed. If anything, I'd have asked him to set the fucker on fire.

Such a jerk….

Bridget and Bernard seemed to think said jerk was the bee's knees, but what the hell? The Silas I had briefly met was about as interesting as a potted plant, as attractive as a ham sandwich, and about as understanding as the Lord of Mordor. I mean—*okay*—he wasn't a total asshat. He'd driven me to a B&B that he probably knew would give me a discount during my stay. But whatever.

I just needed to pay him and get on with my life.

I pulled onto the shoulder, turned the car off, grabbed the bag of food, and climbed out. The sun overhead was bright, the air crisp, and it smelled like fresh grass and wildflowers. The river ahead roared loudly, like it'd been raining a lot the last several days.

I didn't know what river it was, so I pulled my cell out with my free hand to do a quick internet search. The signal dropped to one shaky bar and then the browser refused to load anything.

Are you kidding me?

I wasn't even ten miles outside of Lancaster and it was like the internet ceased to exist. How did these people communicate? Smoke signals?

"It's all the mountains," said a booming voice ahead of me.

I quickly looked up and found a tall, rail-thin, middle-aged man grinning down at me. "Sorry?"

"You got no signal out here because of all the mountains," he reiterated. "Folks got satellite for home internet."

"Satellite? What happens if there's bad weather?" I asked, putting my phone away.

He smiled wider. "No service."

Not that I was in a committed relationship with my phone, but if I was in the mood for mindless scrolling of pretty food and hot guys on Instagram, I damn well expected that feed to load. A man has his needs.

"You from Eatery?"

"Huh? Oh, yeah." I raised the heavy bag.

"Ted Emery," he answered. "I'm the foreman. We've already squared away payment with George."

"All right."

"Go on and hand out the orders, will you?" Ted pointed toward the mouth of the bridge and the group puttering around among equipment. "Don't let none of them give you a hard time." He slapped my shoulder in that weird way dudes sometimes do with each other.

I stumbled forward, clutched the bag tight, and righted myself. God help me if I were to drop the meals of huge, hungry beefcakes who could probably lunge me into the next town like my body was a javelin. A few of the crewmen met me halfway and directed me to a picnic table tucked up against overgrown grasses before the earth sloped down toward the river. One guy, younger than me, followed on my ass and hungrily looked over my shoulder.

"Two, ah—grinders?" I said, reading the handwriting on the outside of each wrapper. I assumed it was New England slang for a sub. "Meatloaf—"

The kid snagged each meal from my hand and called out to the worker who'd ordered it.

"Avocado panini," I continued.

"Ted," the kid called.

"Don't touch my panini," Ted barked from somewhere behind me.

I made eye contact with the kid, hesitated, then set the panini on the tabletop and out of his reach. I went through the rest of the orders with my unrequested assistant's help before taking out the final sandwich and frowning over the note. "Fluffernutter."

The kid laughed and called out, "Silas!"

Silas? Please tell me there's more than one Silas in this town.

I turned quickly and all but knocked into apparently the one and only.

Silas shifted from foot-to-foot and averted his gaze.

You know the earlier thought I'd had about his face and a ham sandwich? Scratch that. That was mean of me. Silas wasn't hiding underneath that beaten-up old cap from yesterday, and his hair had been cut too. His facial scruff was trimmed to a grizzly, manly-man's style, and if I was being honest, I was a fan.

Damn. Silas was actually kind of hot. And still huge. His chest was easily two of me across, and his T-shirt looked about ready to give up and shred into pieces around his biceps. Be still, my heart—I'd be happy to watch him pick up and set down heavy things all day.

Silas finally looked at me again—at least, long enough to point at the sandwich still in my hand.

I glanced down. "Right, sorry. This is yours."

He took it.

"What's a fluffernutter sandwich?"

"Fluff and peanut butter," he said quietly.

"Fluff, like, marshmallow?"

He nodded, turned, and walked away without further word on the subject.

What, Mr. Buff Hot Chest couldn't even say "thank you"? Couldn't at least *pretend* to be a pleasant human? Like, here I was, delivering his lunch, clearly working as promised, and he couldn't—no. He could take his deltoids and grumpy attitude and go build a damn bridge with them. Or whatever he did for a living. He clearly didn't want to make amends or be friends or exchange pleasantries with a gay guy, and that was fine.

Shitty, but fine.

Jerk.

I worked at Eatery until dark. I didn't have anything to do besides go back to the B&B and take a nap or play Candy Crush until my phone died, so I stayed through the dinner rush to pick up extra cash. One of George's part-time cooks made me a sandwich before I clocked out, so I didn't have to worry about feeding myself, which was a bonus. I stepped outside, zipped up my hoodie, and decided to go the opposite way of the Bartholomews and explore more of Lancaster's Main Street.

The temperature dropped a lot around here when the sun went down, but the chill was nice. Sort of refreshing, to be honest. I took extradeep breaths until I felt a little light-headed, each lungful shining light on dark corners inside me. And as I exhaled, that hard lump of *what the fuck am I doing with my life* felt just a little bit smaller.

Which was weird. But I figured it was all this clean air and distance away from LA that was allowing me to regroup. Like I could finally stretch out, relax a bit, not struggle and claw my way to the top for recognition, only to be smacked down by someone better.

Because there was *always* someone more skilled and more talented and more desired. And wasn't that a fucking—

"Hey, kid!"

I startled at the intrusion into my thoughts and stopped walking. I was standing outside a bar, I think. Ah yes, there was the sign.

Bucker's.

Two older men stood underneath it, one completely forgettable and smoking a cigarette, the other overweight and pointing at me while laughing with his buddy.

I frowned and took my hands out of my pockets, in case whatever these drunks wanted, I'd be ready if it came to throwing punches. "What?"

"Some little girl mistake you for a coloring book?" the big one asked.

The smoker laughed louder, started to choke, and thumped on his chest a few times.

Oh, good fucking grief. I rolled my eyes, pushed back the sleeves of my sweatshirt, and said, "Hey, buddy. Let's go get inked together. And while you get a Tinker Bell tramp stamp and cry like a little baby, I'll hold your hand and promise that it looks *so cool*." I smirked and winked for good measure.

He squared his round shoulders and took a drunken step forward. "You think you're stronger than *me*?"

I snorted and took a minute to look him up and down, just to piss him off. "Well, I've had needles drilled into my neck, so yeah." I didn't typically pick fights with drunken strangers, but *a little girl's coloring book*? Do not insult my art.

He motioned for Smoker to follow him—he did not—and started toward me again. Big Guy halted once more when the door to Bucker's opened and loud shitty music poured out onto the quiet street.

And along with it? Silas.

Jesus H. Christ. I got that Lancaster was a small town, but how many times did I have to bump into him before it was considered ridiculous?

Hang on. What had Bridget and Bernard said about this place? Bucker was a homophobic dick and catered to like-minded customers? Well, shit. I guess I *was* right about Silas. It explained why he couldn't even look me in the eye when I spoke.

It figured. The hot ones were always assholes.

Silas hadn't noticed me, completely ignored the two drunks as he left the bar, and studied the ground as he walked away from the building.

The dumbass who thought he wanted to fight me sneered and shouted after Silas, "And don't come back."

Silas raised his head but didn't have the opportunity to turn before stopping short in front of me. "Gideon," he stated, and the inflection of surprise in his tone was the most character I'd heard from him in two days.

"Remembered my name?"

"Of course." He did that foot-to-foot shuffle. "Why are you here?"

"I was taking a walk after work," I answered. "Your buddy stopped me."

Silas did look over his shoulder that time. He shook his head and said to me, "Don't go in there."

"I've no interest. I've already been briefed on the charming shitheads who frequent it." I wasn't trying to start a beef with Silas, but man, I couldn't entirely bite my tongue knowing that I owed money to a guy who hated me for no other reason than I preferred to date men. It bothered me—a lot. "I keep hearing what a good boy you are. Kind of surprised you hang out at Bucker's."

Silas's head snapped up, and he honestly looked taken aback. "I don't. That is—the owner hired me to remove a dead tree from his yard. I came by to get paid."

That was probably the longest and most complete sentence I'd heard since meeting him. And Silas seemed… not insulted, but definitely on the defense.

Was I wrong? Fuck. Wouldn't be the first time.

"Uh—okay. Sorry."

Silas shrugged a shoulder. "It was a job."

"Why don't you both blow each other already?" Smoker finally said, and Big Guy whacked his shoulder and joined him in another round of drunken laughter.

"I bet you want front-row seats," I called back.

"Don't encourage them," Silas said quietly. "They're drunk."

"That's not an excuse for being a righteous piece of shit."

"I know."

Big Guy hurled the next insult, and that time Silas walked toward them. He towered over both idiots, said something out of my earshot, and the two slinked back inside the bar.

"Wow," I said as Silas returned to me. "You're the Homophobe Whisperer."

That got a hesitant almost-smile out of him. "Sorry they bothered you."

"I can defend myself," I replied.

He nodded but said, "This is a nice town."

"It's okay."

"Don't think a few of that sort represent us all."

"Aren't you talkative tonight."

Silas swallowed hard, his Adam's apple bobbing almost painfully. He didn't say anything for a minute.

Then it all suddenly came together, like the final piece of a puzzle completing the image.

Awkward. Shy—insanely shy. And maybe… *interested*.

"Can I walk you home?" Silas asked, his voice barely reaching above a whisper.

"What?"

"Nothing. Never mind," he said quickly, shaking his head.

"No—I, uh—I guess so," I answered. "If you want to."

I turned in the direction of the B&B, and Silas fell into step beside me without a word. We walked past Eatery, a café, the so, so sad one-room theater, and Silas still hadn't said anything. I looked sideways at him. He didn't seem at all concerned with social norms like small talk. Maybe he, quite literally, just wanted to *walk* with me. But me—I couldn't stand not talking.

"You got a haircut."

He nodded.

"Looks good. Yesterday you had a bit of a Sasquatch thing going on."

Silas cleared his throat. "Maybe a little."

"So you fix bridges?"

"Restoration," he corrected.

"Do you like it?"

"Yes."

I looked at Silas again. "Come on, Chatty Cathy. Tell me *why* you like it."

He hesitated, his mouth working at trying to find the words. "Covered bridges are important to our local heritage and a source of income during tourist season."

"Ah. So you're the sort who likes to help, are you?"

"Is that bad?"

"Nope."

There was no more conversation until we'd put the dinky antique shop behind us and turned off Main Street.

Silas asked suddenly, "What did you do in California?"

"Dead-end shit that got me nowhere. I quit my job."

"I see."

"I worked at a tattoo parlor."

"I wouldn't have guessed."

I snorted and laughed. "Do I detect sarcasm? Wow. All right, touché. I started an apprenticeship under the owner. He does amazing work." I held my hands out and showed Silas. One sported a rose, the other the lower portion of a human skull. "But there's always someone bigger and better than you in LA."

"Is there?"

"It's a pretty cutthroat city, no matter the industry. Someone else's skills ended up rocking his world and… here I am. I stuck around for a while, but I wasn't looking to be a tattoo parlor receptionist for the rest of my life. Anyway, it's a sob story that ends up with me totaling two cars and screaming obscenities at a moose."

Silas chuckled.

We reached the B&B a few minutes later, and Silas stopped first. His eyes were all over the place—my forehead to my hands down to his feet. He was acting like a nervous teenager returning from their first damn date—oh my God, was Silas hoping for some tongue? But before I could give him a nudge and a tease….

"Good night," Silas said quickly before turning and walking back the way we'd come.

CHAPTER THREE

"Hell."

I stopped in the kitchen doorway at Eatery, bin in hand, and watched George hang up the phone. "Everything okay?"

He was grinding his teeth as he turned to me. "That was the school. My little girl just projectile vomited in gym class and needs to be picked up."

The phone rang again.

George pointed at it. "And the lunch orders are coming in."

"I got it," Nancy said, doing an impressive spin maneuver to grab the phone on her way by the counter. "Eatery."

I shifted the bin to rest on my hip. "Wife?" I tried.

George shook his head, already untying his apron. "She's a nurse at the hospital."

"The part-time cook from last night. What's his name—"

"He's got a day job." George pulled the apron over his head, paused, and looked at me with a sudden glint in his eye. "Can you cook?"

"Me? No, no, no. Ask Nancy."

George glanced sideways as Nancy hung up the phone before greeting two patrons at the door. "I love her to death, honest, but she can hardly boil an egg. I'm serious, Gideon. Can you cook?"

"I, uh—I mean, I guess so."

"That's what I want to hear. Come with me."

I followed George into the kitchen, set the bin down on the dishwashing counter, and headed to the range. He performed the world's shittiest tour of the area—fire, knives, food—then motioned to the tickets already tucked into the holder above the prep counter.

"These are for the Bridge. Get them done and let Nancy know when you're leaving to make the delivery. I'll be back as soon as I can." George was out the back door of the kitchen in a matter of seconds.

I let out a breath and checked the tickets. They all seemed reasonable-enough meals to cobble together. George's style was high quality and healthy comfort foods. Sandwiches, chili, casserole, soup—which he'd already pulled together from scratch that morning, along with the daily desserts—so, cool. I could do this.

And I did. In fact, I was ready to pat myself on the back before giving pause to the final order on the list.

Fluffernutter sandwich.

Good Christ, Silas.

I'd mentioned in passing, upon my return from the delivery yesterday, that it seemed odd for a grown man to be eating nothing but pure sugar and peanut butter. I mean, it seemed like it'd be a popular snack with the afternoon cartoons crowd, not a guy who I guessed was flirting with thirty at the minimum.

George had simply replied that Silas was a well-known picky eater in town and there was nothing to be done about it.

Maybe Silas simply didn't like hearty New England meals. And maybe he'd never tried anything else. Maybe he just needed a push in the right foodie direction....

"What's this?" Silas asked when I handed him a take-out container.

"Lunch."

He glanced up from the scribbled note on the lid. "I ordered a sandwich."

I raised a skeptical brow. "Yeah, about that... do you know how many calories are in a single serving of that marshmallow fluff?"

"About damn time he gets called out," said one of Silas's coworkers sitting at the picnic table. "We tell him every day he's going to eventually drop dead from those sandwiches. It's that or corned beef and cabbage. All he eats."

"That's not true," Silas murmured. His cheeks had a distinct dusting of pink on them.

Holy shit, he was blushing.

I crossed my arms and tilted my head to catch Silas's downcast expression. "George had to run out, so I helped with lunch. I made you fish tacos. Tilapia. Do you like that? George doesn't have any shrimp. The salsa is canned, too, because I didn't have time to make my own."

Silas popped open the container to stare at the contents.

"It's one of my favorite recipes," I finished.

I wasn't sure if his silence was the normal kind, or if he was so beyond disgusted that Silas was simply trying to keep it together enough to not have a stroke. I glanced over his shoulder at the table to see several of the burly construction guys watching with varying levels of interest.

Uh....

"So I'm going to leave now," I stated.

Silas cleared his throat and looked at me again. "Thank you for lunch."

"Sure."

The seated guys grumbled under their breaths and exchanged dollar bills.

I made a hasty retreat to the delivery car. My stomach was getting weird and flippy-floppy, and I didn't know why. I was only here to make a delivery. I gave a sexy countryman his taco lunch. That was all. Yes, of course, tacos paved the way to anyone's heart but—

Wait a minute.

I was flirting with Silas? Upon realizing last night that he was quite likely the strong and stoic local gay man, was I, like… interested in him or something?

Was I using tacos as a means of wooing him?

Oh my God.

The fuck was wrong with me? Silas was *so* not my type. Too much flannel, not enough ink, and what the hell was even his last name? He seemed too naïve and too innocent. The guys I usually gave The Look to were colorful and punky and arrogant and sometimes promiscuous and—

I banged my forehead against the steering wheel.

Wow.

I was a mess.

Maybe the fresh air around here was *too* fresh. That must have been it. Too much oxygen was making me bat my lashes at the guy who just two days ago I'd wanted to strangle for seemingly having no sympathy or understanding. Except... he kind of did. In his own awkward way, Silas cared.

I shook my head, started the car, and pulled away from the Bridge.

I was only passing through.

There was no plan to stick around for a minute longer than necessary.

And yet—I couldn't shake the giddy hopefulness that Silas would like my cooking above everyone else's.

And that maybe he... I don't know, thought I was kinda cute.

I was growing fond of mornings in Lancaster.

I stood on the back patio of the B&B with a hot cup of coffee, a cool sweetness in the air, and birds chirping and eating in the nearby feeders. I sipped and studied the tree line across the lawn. This far up north, in such an isolated area, those trees were an actual forest. A forest with bears and deer and shit in there.

City-boy me was admittedly a little unnerved by the idea of wild animals being *right there*, but the locals weren't fazed in the slightest. I figured they all survived this long, so I'd have to trust Bridget when she slapped my arm, laughed, and said, "Oh, they won't hurt you, babycakes."

A breeze rustled one of Bridget's purple wind chimes hanging from the roof, adding tranquil music to the otherwise silent day.

I closed my eyes.

Was Silas awake? Probably. I bet he was one of those early, the-sun-isn't-even-up-yet risers. Maybe he even stood outside like this too.

"Good morning!"

I jumped and spilled coffee all over myself. "Shit."

"Oops, sorry about that, honey," Bridget said from behind me.

I turned, wiping at my shirt. "It's fine."

She motioned for me from the open doorway. "Come inside for a second."

I frowned, flicked the coffee from my hand, and followed Bridget into the house. "What is it?" I asked as we walked down the hall to the foyer.

She moved behind the counter and opened the big ledger. "There's a small problem with your room."

Motherfucker.

"It seems like Bernard double-booked."

"What's that mean?"

Bridget hummed to herself as she flipped through the pages. "Yeah… uh-huh. Okay. So we have a family arriving today who booked and paid for your room a month ago."

"That's fine. I'll take another room."

Bridget glanced up while twirling a lock of purple hair. "We're full-up, angel."

Son of a bitch.

I set the almost-empty mug down on the counter and managed to ask with a relatively chill tone, "For how long?"

"Nothing opens up again until next week."

Shit, fuck, cock, hell.

Bridget's eyes brightened and she waved both hands suddenly. "There's an inn just up the road. They're bound to have availability. And then you can come back here," she said happily. "I promise it's not double-booked after that."

The inn was going to be more expensive. Even if Bridget refunded me for my unused nights, it wasn't going to be enough for a week at a fancy little mountain resort. I wasn't scheduled to be paid at Eatery until the end of the week either. Maybe I could ask George to spot me....

"I'm sorry, sweetie," Bridget murmured.

I put on a brave face and said, "Don't worry about it." I was screaming internally, but I couldn't find it within myself to be angry at a cute old lady with purple hair. Bridget was nice. It wasn't her fault Bernard needed a stronger vision prescription.

I went upstairs after that bomb drop. I had meant to at least change out of my coffee-covered shirt, but to no one's surprise, I had no clean clothes and had neglected to utilize the B&B's laundry services last night. So, looking like I needed to wear a bib, I packed up my bag and vacated the pink wonderland. I walked to Eatery with my duffel slung over one shoulder and practiced how I'd ask George for an advance without sounding super pathetic.

Could it get any worse?

But I should have known better than to even *think* that question.

Tempting fate—that's what that was.

The front door of Eatery slammed open as I reached for the handle, and I was smacked in the face.

"Son of a fuck," I shouted, toppling backward and landing on my ass. My glasses fell off and blood dripped from my nose.

"*Uh-oh*," said a kid's voice before the door banged shut.

I picked up my glasses and put them on as the door opened, more gently, a second time.

"Gideon," George exclaimed in surprise. "Are you okay?"

"No," I grumbled. I took George's outstretched hand, grabbed my bag, and got to my feet.

"You got a bloody nose, boyo."

"Yup." I carefully touched my face, and my fingers came away bright red.

George ushered me inside, pushed me onto an empty stool at the counter, and handed me a wad of napkins. "Ellen." His voice managed to boom without actually having to yell. "Come over here right now and apologize, missy."

I glanced sideways as footsteps scuffled across the linoleum floor. A little girl stopped beside me and looked up. She was wearing a bright, *bright, bright* pink princess dress and a Batman facemask.

"I'm sorry I hit your face," she stated bluntly.

"Thanks."

"Can I see your hand?" she asked next, clearly not all that interested in my bloody nose or being remorseful for what she'd done.

I held my hand out.

She traced the outline of my skull tattoo with her tiny finger. "Did this hurt?"

"A little. Were you the one who barfed in gym class yesterday?"

Ellen nodded. "On Mrs. W's sneakers," she clarified. "I had milk at snack time. Then Mrs. W made me run, and I said, '*No way*. I don't run after chocolate milk, Mrs. W.' And she said, 'Ellen, Ellen, Ellen. I blew my whistle—that means you run.' So I said, 'Okay, but it might be bad....'"

"And it *was* bad."

Ellen nodded again. "It smelled gross."

"*Ellen*," George said with a hand over his face. "Go color."

She let go of my hand and skipped to one of the booths in the back of the restaurant where she'd set up shop.

"There's no school today," George said as he looked back at me. "Sorry about that. What's with the bag? You're not leaving town, are you?"

"No," I said, wondering if I had heard disappointment in George's voice or simply hoped I had. "The B&B overbooked, so I have to stay somewhere else for a week."

George made a face. "Where?"

"I guess the inn Bridget suggested." I wimped out of asking for my paycheck just then. I simply couldn't do it, not while wearing coffee stains and sporting a bloody nose, courtesy of Batman. "I'll figure it out."

"You've got some coffee on you," George said after a minute.

"I know."

"Long morning?"

"You can say that."

George chuckled and asked, "So I guess cooking went okay yesterday?"

I straightened. "Yeah. I mean, did someone complain or something?"

George patted his apron pockets and pulled out a few tickets. "The Bridge called in their lunch order just before you came in. Half of them are for fish tacos. Including Silas. Which I have to say is… unexpected. I have to make him the same four meals. He won't eat anything else. How'd you trick him?"

I laughed a little and smiled. "He wanted another one of those nasty nutterfluff—"

"Fluffernutter."

"*Fluffernutter* sandwiches," I said. "And I thought, he's a big guy and probably needs something with more protein if he's going to be working outside all day. Did he *really* like the tacos?"

George nodded. "Yup."

"I kind of had fun cooking," I continued. "If you need any help—I could make something different."

"For Silas? You're playing with fire."

"I think I might be figuring his palate out."

George looked skeptical but indulgent.

"I make a killer burger. Have you ever had kimchi on a burger?"

"Can't say I have."

"Cross my heart it's the best damn topping you'll ever taste on a beef patty."

George narrowed his eyes, now suspicious.

"If you've got cabbage and rice vinegar, I can make some now. It'll be ready by lunch."

George grinned after a beat, pointed a thick finger at me, and said, "Tell you what. If Silas eats kimchi and likes it, I'll let you come up with the daily special for tomorrow."

"Really?"

"Sure. You like cooking, and you're not too bad at it—what do I have to lose?"

I loved food almost as much as I did tattooing. And food was probably the one real thing I had been missing about LA. The food trucks, desserts like macaroon ice cream sandwiches, and the ability to order bubble tea and have it delivered at midnight. Not that Eatery was bad. George really *was* a talented chef, and sometimes nothing hit the spot like a shepherd's pie recipe passed down through the generations. But I liked cooking new and interesting things, so not only would it be a welcomed change from carting dirty dishes around, but the notion that folks would enjoy *my* creations?

My battered ego perked up in delight.

"Here you are." I handed Silas his lunch. "It's not tacos."

"Oh. It's not?"

I grinned at the note of disappointment. "Heard you liked them, though."

He shrugged. Nodded. "They were different." He popped open the container.

I leaned closer and pointed. "George said you usually eat burgers that are as well-done as an old boot. I'm sorry to disappoint, but I can't in good conscience do that to meat. It's medium. Give it a try before you toss it."

Silas was still staring at the food. "What's that on top?"

"Kimchi."

"I don't—"

"Have you *had* kimchi?" I asked over him.

Silas glanced sideways at me. "No," he said at length.

"One bite. Just try it." I nodded my chin at the picnic table. "There's an extra taco order for you if you really hate the burger."

"No one else got this?"

"I made it special for you."

Silas quickly closed the carton and cleared his throat. "That's very kind. Thank you."

"Can I ask you something?"

"Okay."

I crossed my arms and didn't break eye contact with Silas. "Why are all your crew dudes watching us and making bets?"

His face colored. "Don't worry about them."

"Come on. What's the game? Can I get in on it?"

"It's stupid."

"I'm willing to chance it."

Silas looked down and plucked absently at the corner of the container. "I like you," he said bluntly.

I slowly lowered my arms. "You do?"

"Yes."

"*Why?*"

Silas raised his head, looking surprised by the question.

And realizing how self-deprecating I sounded, I quickly said, "Never mind. You're not half bad yourself, Mountain Man."

"I'm not?"

"So what's the bet?"

Silas glanced at the picnic table and the crew members thoroughly invested in our conversation. "Whether or not I'll kiss you."

"Split fifty-fifty?" I asked.

"Sixty-forty."

"I brought you delicious food and you get to kiss these lips," I countered, tapping the side of my mouth. "It should be sixty-forty in my favor."

"Fine. Fifty-fifty."

I smirked. "All right. So come on."

Silas's mouth worked, but he didn't draw closer.

"Does it count if I kiss you?" I prompted.

"No. I need to do it."

"I've got a job, bud. I can't wait all day," I teased. "Don't let the scruff and tattoos scare you off."

"I like them," Silas answered before taking a bold step closer.

"You've kissed a guy before, right?"

"Yeah."

"Okay. Just checking," I said. "Oh. Tongue or no tongue?"

"No tongue."

"Continue."

Silas laughed. A sweet and gentle sound, with a smile, rarely seen, that turned out to match. He leaned down and pressed his mouth to mine.

I briefly heard some guys protest at having lost the bet, but otherwise my attention was all on Silas. His lips were surprisingly soft—tasting like coffee and spring air—and his facial hair tugged lightly against my own. Silas smelled like a simple soap, the great outdoors, and all man.

He pulled away and said, "Thanks for lunch."

"Huh… y-yeah. Sure."

Silas smiled shyly, then rejoined the crew.

CHAPTER FOUR

"Gideon, got a minute?"

I'd been on my way out for the night when George called me to the counter. "What's up?" I asked.

"I found you an alternative to the inn." George handed me a slip of paper.

"Really?" I glanced at the address scribbled in George's heavy-handed chicken scratch.

"I was talking to my younger brother earlier. I mentioned your predicament, and he offered to let you crash on his couch."

"I don't want to impose on your family."

George waved his hand. "My brother wouldn't have offered if he wasn't serious. So I don't see it as an imposition. Unless you had your heart set on paying for the inn."

"Definitely not."

George grinned. "Then stay with him. He's a good guy—lives in Dalton, though—you'll need to take the delivery car."

"What?"

Is he fucking with me?

George looked confused.

"I can borrow the car too?"

"You sure as hell can't use yours."

"Well, no…."

"Then drive safe—it's dark out," he said, handing me the car keys.

I was honestly taken aback by the small-town generosity. I'd never experienced this *we got your back* mentality so much in my entire life. Sure, my reason for initially being in Lancaster blew, but Silas had my car towed for free, the B&B gave me a discount for an extended stay without my asking, George hired me on the spot and trusted me not to fuck up his kitchen, and now his brother—who I didn't even know—was letting me stay for free at his house?

"This is really nice of you," I said. "Thanks. That sounds cheap, but I mean it."

George just smiled. "See you tomorrow."

I said good night to him and the rest of the evening staff before ducking out. The drive took me on the same one road that was my usual route to the Bridge, but this time I took the left turn and continued on toward Dalton. The radio murmured quietly, keeping me company on the long empty stretch of country road. There was nothing out here but trees, moose-crossing signs, and the occasional lone house. It was so isolated and different from the world I grew up in. I shifted uncomfortably and shrugged off the odd sensation of *coming home*.

The road ran along the river I still hadn't looked up the name of, dipping dangerously close at times, with only a feeble guardrail to keep drivers on the asphalt and not taking a swim instead. Eventually I reached another fork, with a road sign indicating Whitefield to the left and Dalton straight ahead. An old railroad bridge spanned the dark water and disappeared into the shady trees beyond.

There were more scatterings of houses out this way. I drove by an itty-bitty firehouse, a building advertising itself as the town hall, one church—denomination unknown— and that seemed to be it. I glanced in the rearview mirror, watching the hub of Dalton disappear in the taillights.

"That was it?" I asked. "*That* was Dalton?"

No traffic light.

Not even a *caution light*.

I put the scrap of paper on the steering wheel and glanced at the writing again. George had helpfully provided a few directions.

Drive past firehouse.

About a mile or so after the Shop on the Hill.

Union Road on your left.

I snorted. I guess I should have expected those kinds of directions after being told *just drive* to find the Bridge, but yeah.

About a mile or so. Okay.

Luckily, I did pass a small store, and it *was* on top of a hill, so I must have been on the right path. There was also a lone gas station—already closed for the night. I kept going, and when I feared I was totally fucking lost, I saw a green sign advertising Union Road. It was dark as I made my way down, the only illumination coming from the few houses along either side. I eventually spotted a mailbox with the house number I was looking for and pulled into the driveway.

The home was a log cabin. Like an actual log cabin a mountaineer would live in. I didn't even know people outside of HGTV actually lived in these. But it was nice. Probably worth a small fortune, if the amount of untouched land surrounding it was any indication.

I shut the car off, grabbed my bag, and climbed out. The front door opened as I started up the walkway, and a big husky ran out to greet me. It barked, wagged its tail, and ran speedy circles around me.

"He's friendly."

I whipped around from trying to pet the dog and to the familiar voice. Sure as shit, there was Silas standing in the open doorway. "What—*you're* George's brother?"

Silas nodded and leaned against the threshold.

"Why didn't you tell me?"

"You didn't ask."

I rolled my eyes and huffed loud enough that he heard it. "Is it a problem?"

"*No.* So… Silas Bright? It's a cute name, I guess," I grumbled before asking, "Did you really offer to let me stay, or did George ask you?"

"I offered." He straightened and took a step to the side. "Coming?"

I walked to the door, the dog running ahead and disappearing inside. "You live alone?"

Silas shut the door quietly behind me. "Yes."

I quickly toed off my Chucks and stepped into the wide-open living room. I whistled and set my bag down on the couch. Just in front of the furniture was a fireplace and a widescreen television mounted above it on the wall. Toward the immediate left was a sliding-glass door—blinds drawn. Farther behind me to the left was what I guessed was a bathroom and a closed door, probably Silas's bedroom.

On the opposite end of the room was a small dining table situated under another shuttered window, currently piled with junk and looking unused.

It was rustic, sure, but comfortable.

Warm.

"Nice place," I stated.

"Hungry?"

I turned around. Goddammit, how did Silas look so hot in ratty jeans and flannel? Manly men like him had never been my thing, nor had grunge boys, so I had no idea why plaid was getting me all hot and bothered.

"Dinner's almost ready." He moved to the right, passed by the dining table, and vanished around a corner.

I hesitantly followed and found Silas in a cramped kitchen. The fridge had a few photos held up with magnets—Silas and George, another of a woman who I presumed was his sister-in-law, and his little niece, Ellen. There were a lot of pictures of him and Ellen, actually. Figures that Silas, the good boy, was also a perfect uncle. Pushed against the wall in the back of the kitchen was a smaller table—set for two people.

Smooth.

I didn't comment on that and instead said, "Your niece is adorable."

"She's a gem," Silas replied, stirring something in a pot on the stove.

"I met her this morning. She was dressed like Princess Batman."

"Sounds about right."

"Can I help with anything?"

"No. Take a seat." Silas nodded at the table before he began scooping out the contents into two bowls beside him on the counter.

I sat down as instructed. "What's on the menu?"

"American chop suey."

"Uh-huh. And what's that?"

Silas brought the bowls over and slid one in front of me. "Tomato sauce, hamburger—er, ground beef—onion, and elbow noodles."

"Sounds like spaghetti that tried and gave up."

Silas smiled a little and took the seat across from me. "Guess so."

"Is this what you like?"

Silas dug his fork into the bowl, glanced up, and gave me a curious expression.

"New England comfort food," I clarified.

He shrugged. "Oh. Well. Mama was a picky eater. I guess I never learned much else." Silas stared at me again. "I, um… I like your cooking, though. I can't make anything so fancy."

I almost laughed that he thought fish tacos and kimchi were fancy, but Silas looked both dead serious and a bit embarrassed. I knew in that half a second I had to choke on air; if I'd laughed, he'd have shut down.

"Thank you. So did you eat the burger?"

Silas's cheeks darkened and he stuffed a forkful of chop suey in his mouth before nodding. "I liked it," he said between chews. "It was… unique."

"I'm glad you tried it."

Silas shrugged one shoulder and asked before taking another large bite, "Why were you driving through New Hampshire?"

"Midlife crisis."

He raised an eyebrow.

"I'm twenty-five," I clarified. "But I figured, might as well get that breakdown out of the way while I'm young and have a chance of bouncing back."

He covered his mouth and coughed before managing to swallow his food.

I grinned. "You okay?"

"Fine."

"I guess I needed to find myself. After I quit my job at the parlor, I subleased my apartment to a buddy, packed a bag, and took off. I was going to drive all the way to Maine before making my way back to California. Saying that out loud sounds melodramatic, but… LA was so claustrophobic. I couldn't breathe. I couldn't… do anything right."

"I'm sorry."

"It's not your fault. Anyway, *I* should be sorry. You don't need to know all of this crap."

"Sometimes it's good to talk," Silas said. "Get it out of your system."

"Says the guy who speaks about five words every time I see him," I teased.

He shifted in his chair and glanced between me and his food. "But I talk when I need to."

"I'm more than capable of filling any silences," I said with a laugh before finally trying a bite.

Oh God. Oh God.

The food was awful.

Silas was not a good cook.

I managed to swallow, despite every reflex wanting me to spit it out.

Unfortunately, he noticed. "Is it no good?"

"Ah… it's okay." I took another tiny bite, as if to prove a point.

"George is the chef, not me," Silas explained. "I won't be offended."

I forced down a few more bites, for no other reason than I was hungry and didn't want to be a complete ass. "I'll cook tomorrow," I offered, trying to hide the hopeful note in my voice.

He immediately brightened. "Tacos?"

"I've never left New Hampshire," Silas said as he rinsed our bowls in the sink after I'd finished telling him about a visit I'd made to Darwin, Minnesota—a town of a few hundred residents and one exceptionally large ball of twine.

"I'd never left California until now," I answered in agreement. "Not that I'd planned on taking this trip, but it's been nice seeing the country."

"Roadside attractions."

"I guess. I also saw the world's biggest boot in Minnesota. Twenty-foot tall Red Wing."

"Folks must be bored in Minnesota," Silas said as he reached for a hand towel.

"So you've never been tempted to break a world record while kickin' it up here in Small Town, USA?"

"Not personally." Silas set the towel aside and looked at me. "New Hampshire was in the Guinness World Records, though."

"For what?"

"A ten-foot corpse flower grown in Gilford."

"*Wow*," I said, sort of… just…. "That's *exciting*."

Silas shrugged.

I stood up. "Can I use the bathroom?"

"Sure." He pointed. "Past the front door on the left."

I excused myself, pet the big husky in the doorway, and found the bathroom on the other end of the house. Inside, I took off my glasses, set them on the counter, and splashed my face with cold water until I was gasping for air. Dinner—despite being nearly inedible—had been great. I mean, sitting with Silas and not feeling like I had to be *on* for him to like me. He liked my smart mouth the way it was, seemed to enjoy listening to me talk and talk and talk…. And his home felt like—he felt like—

I splashed my face a final time.

"Dumbass," I said to myself. I wiped my face dry with the corner of my shirt and stepped out.

The house sounded empty. I looked toward the kitchen, and the dog was no longer in the doorway. I glanced at the sliding-glass door and noticed the blinds had been pulled aside enough to slip outside. I grabbed my Chucks, hopped foot-to-foot while pulling them on, walked across the living room, and opened the door.

"Can I join you?" I asked, poking my head out.

Silas was lounging in one of two chairs on the patio. "Yes," he said, not looking over his shoulder.

I moved to the chair beside his and sat. I studied his profile, weakly illuminated by the interior lights glowing on the other side of the glass door. "I never pegged you as the smoking sort."

Silas quickly snuffed out a cigarette in an ashtray near his foot. "I'm not. Not really. When I'm nervous."

"What're you nervous about?"

Silas let a moment pass without response. He rested a tumbler on his knee, his huge hand making it look like a child's play toy. "It's been a while since I've been interested in a guy." He finally looked at me. "Since the interest has been returned."

My face warmed. "So you're out?"

Silas took a sip of what looked like whiskey, then nodded. "Not a lot of pickings in a small town, though."

"Guess not."

"I don't mean to sound desperate. I've had boyfriends before. Our meeting felt serendipitous, is all."

"I hit your car."

"I'm well aware."

I snorted and then burst out laughing. "Your sarcasm is on-point."

Silas was grinning when he offered his tumbler to me.

I accepted it, took a sip, then said, "You don't know me, though. What if you end up hating me?"

"No one knows each other in the beginning."

"*And* he's poetic," I said loudly to the dark woodlands surrounding us.

"I like… talking to you," Silas said, hesitating like he'd just come clean about committing some heinous crime. "I don't feel comfortable around most people."

"But you do with me?"

Silas nodded, still studying me.

"What next, then?"

The husky came bounding out of the tree line, carrying a bona fide *log* in his mouth, tail wagging with pure doggy joy. He set the treasure down on the patio stairs and looked up at us.

"I'd like to take you out."

"Like on a date?"

"Does it imply otherwise?"

I laughed again. "I've never been asked out so formally. It's nice, to be honest. I'll even wear my shirt *without* the coffee stains."

"Sounds serious," he said, and then we were both laughing again like teenagers.

If this is what happiness was—pure and unadulterated—sign me up.

"Do you mind if we take it slow?" Silas asked after a calm settled between us. "For me. Getting my toes wet again and all."

"No, I don't mind," I said. "Actually, I'd like that too. Usually I jump into bed first, ask questions second, and then two weeks later wonder why I'm fucking single."

He stood suddenly. "Have you looked up yet?"

"Have I what?"

"I'm being literal."

"I suspected as much."

Silas held a hand out, took the tumbler from mine, set it aside, then dragged me from the chair. He led me down the steps and into the yard, put his hands on my shoulders, and turned me away from the light of the house. "Look up."

So I did.

And I saw stars.

Not the handfuls that managed to blink through the light-polluted skies of urban landscapes either, but thousands. *Millions*. A massive streak of them tore across the sky over Silas's home like an old battle scar aged white with time.

"That's the Milky Way."

"Jesus fucking Christ."

"I think *this* is why I'd miss New Hampshire if I left."

"I've never seen so many stars. I can even see constellations!"

Silas placed a hesitant and gentle kiss to the back of my head. He moved one hand from my shoulder, down my arm, and cautiously slid his fingers between mine.

His grip was firm, warm… a *foundation*.

CHAPTER FIVE

I'd learned the night before that the husky's name was Ben.

And Ben woke me with a high-pitched whine and then plenty of slobbery licks to my face. I sat up on the couch and wiped my cheeks and mouth. "Dammit, Ben… *gross*. What do you want?"

"His morning walk."

I turned around as Silas was stepping out of his bedroom. I grabbed my glasses from the coffee table and put them on just as he finished tugging a shirt over his head. I caught a sneak peek of tanned skin and abs so defined that I could scrub laundry on them.

Yes, please.

I belatedly realized that Silas was staring at me too and I suddenly felt *very* naked. The bare tattooed skin of my chest and stomach pebbled from the chill while my face warmed simultaneously under his gaze. I figured all the ink was a lot to take in.

Silas nodded once to himself and continued toward the front door. "Pretty," he said under his breath.

I stumbled to my feet while asking, "What's pretty?"

He waved a hand in my direction as he put his shoes on. "Your tattoos."

"All of them?"

"All of them." Silas collected a leash hanging on the wall near the front door. "Want to join us?"

"Before coffee? Or a shower? Your neighbors will judge me."

"No one out there but Mrs. Murphy on her morning jog."

"Could I at least throw my clothes in your washer first? I've got nothing to wear today."

Silas returned to the couch and held his hands out.

"What?"

"Give me your clothes."

"Your first glimpse of my underwear won't be from pawing through my dirty laundry, good sir."

Silas didn't move and instead just looked even more expectant.

"You're killing me, Mountain Man," I whined.

"It's time efficient. I'll start the laundry, you put a shirt on, and we can go for a walk before Ben tap dances his toes off."

I leaned to one side, looked around Silas's looming figure, and watched the dog wiggle and shake at the door. I sighed, reached down, and grabbed the bag from beside the couch. I reluctantly handed it over and watched Silas take it to a door near the bathroom. He flipped a light switch in the small room and started moving about. I grabbed my shirt from yesterday, put it on, detoured to the bathroom long enough to relieve myself and brush my teeth, then joined Silas.

We stepped outside into the crisp, cool morning air. Dew practically glowed on the assortment of flowers planted along the walkway. The rising sun cast a clear, clean light over the surrounding woodland—the green so green that it was sort of like being in the Land of Oz.

Ben was given plenty of lead on his leash, and he trotted happily ahead of us down Union Road.

"Where're you taking me on our date?" I asked at length.

"What do you enjoy?"

I shrugged and bumped Silas's shoulder with mine. "The classic?"

"Dinner and a movie?"

"Sure."

"Children's movie at the theater this week."

"Right, the one-room movie theater. So just dinner, then. What sort of cheap options are we looking at?"

"It's my treat," Silas answered, then held up a hand when I took an intake of air to protest. After a moment, he scratched the side of his nose nervously. "There's a nice place in Lancaster—The Pier. It's mostly seafood." He said that last comment with a bit of a grumble.

"You don't like seafood?"

Silas shook his head.

"You ate those fish tacos I made, though."

"Because you made them."

I smiled and nudged Silas's shoulder again. "You're so damn charming. Has anyone told you that?"

"I'll pick you up after your shift at Eatery."

Back home—Silas's house, that was—he hopped in the shower and I tossed my clothes in the dryer. I went to the kitchen next, made a pot of coffee, and took a moment to snoop through Silas's cupboards. Not much in the way of ingredients, so homemade pancakes for breakfast was out of the question. But hey, thank God he had a huge tub of both peanut butter and that sticky marshmallow fluff.

I tried the fridge next and was a bit luckier on that front. I pulled out a few eggs, an onion, and a lone bell pepper that looked as if Silas had bought it without any clue as to what to do with it and then intended on leaving it to wither and die in the crisper. I chopped the veggies, whipped the eggs, and poured them into a pan on the stovetop when Silas appeared in the kitchen doorway in my peripheral vision.

"What smells good?"

"Omelets," I answered, carefully folding the eggs. "Although, to be technical, the smell is sautéed onions. All you need to do to trick someone into thinking you're a master chef is to sauté some onion and maybe garlic—" I turned toward Silas and immediately forgot what I was talking about when I was met with bare man chest packed with muscle atop muscle.

Silas put both arms through the sleeves of his shirt and stared back at me. "What?"

"*What?*"

"You were saying something about onions."

The sizzle of the omelet caught my attention, and I quickly turned off the burner. "I've forgotten." I looked at Silas again. "Would you call that a six-pack?"

Silas looked down at his abs before quickly yanking the T-shirt over his head and covering himself.

"Or an eight-pack?" I concluded.

"Sorry."

"Oh no, the eye candy is much appreciated." I cut the omelet in two with the edge of the spatula and slid half onto an awaiting plate. "Here you go. I'm going to shower real quick."

"What about yours?" Silas asked, motioning to the stove as I moved around him.

"My grubbiness trumps hot eggs. But you eat."

I headed into the bathroom and found that Silas had left a folded towel on the edge of the sink beside my kit of toiletries. I stripped out of yesterday's clothes, turned on the taps, and got in under the steam and scalding heat, and it felt amazing. Afterward, I'd barely wrapped the towel around my waist when I heard something plop down on the floor in front of the bathroom. I cracked the door open and saw it was a laundry basket.

"I didn't look at your underwear," Silas called, already halfway back to the kitchen.

I bent down and sifted through the clothes. "Everything's folded."

"I closed my eyes."

I smirked. Silas Bright was charming and domestic and decent and a little bit of a smartass. I settled on a pair of purple checkered pants—which my ass looked fucking fine in, thank you very much—and a black button-down. I'd still need to use an apron at work if I wanted to wear this attire to dinner tonight, but should I spill or walk into something, because this *was* me, after all, at least stains wouldn't show up as easily on dark colors. I returned to the kitchen while rolling back the cuffs of my shirt.

"So how was the omelet?"

Silas offered me a cup of coffee. "Good."

"Yeah?" I accepted the mug and took a drink. "You didn't slip it to the dog, did you?"

Silas cracked a smile, moved away from the counter he was leaning against, and showed an empty plate beside the sink with only a few pieces of green pepper that'd been picked out and left behind. He then grabbed my plate, stared at the food, then awkwardly pointed at the microwave on the opposite counter.

"Sure, that's fine. Thanks."

Silas put it in, pressed a button, and said over the hum, while watching the plate turn, "You look nice."

I paused midsip, swallowed, managed to somehow choke, then wheezed, "Do I?"

He nodded and added, "I really like your tattoos."

"I stand out just a bit in these parts."

Silas took the plate out of the microwave and handed it to me. He pointed at my left arm and asked, "Is that a dragon? What's it mean? Or is that a stupid tattoo question?"

"There are no stupid questions," I replied. I put the plate on the counter, along with my mug, before rolling the sleeve back to my elbow. "I wanted something that would represent strength, and I wanted it big and bright because it'd be uncomfortable to sit through all that shading and coloring."

"A literal reminder of strength?"

"*Yeah*," I said, smiling. "Exactly. If I can sit through getting my elbow done, which hurts like a bitch, mind you, then I'm stronger than what my brain tries to tell me sometimes." I rubbed at the ink and added, "And I chose the pride colors because *obviously*."

"Obviously," Silas echoed. He took my hand and gave it a firm squeeze.

George stood with his back to the stoves in the kitchen, a shit-eating grin on his face as I came through the door.

"What?" I asked, tying my apron.

"Nice threads."

"Thanks."

"Have plans tonight?"

"You're hilarious. Why didn't you tell me that Silas was your brother?"

"You didn't ask," George replied.

"That's what he said," I retorted before leaning over the prep table between us. "You set me up."

George laughed loudly. "Are you complaining?"

I was getting warm again, and it had nothing to do with the temperature of the kitchen. "Well… no."

"Silas called me yesterday after he kissed you."

"He told you about that?"

George motioned me to join him at the stoves. "He made fifty bucks off the Bridge boys."

"Half of that is mine," I countered.

George shuffled through the tickets he'd been holding in one hand. "Anyway, I'd mentioned your mix-up with the Bartholomews, and that's when he offered his couch." He handed me a few of the lunch orders. "You like him?"

I cleared my throat. "Yeah."

"I know he's big and burly and can probably deadlift a car, but Silas is a sweet kid. Be good to him, okay?" George fixed me with a stare so strong, it was like a bullet shot straight through the chest.

"S-sure. I mean, I will. *Yes*," I said, stumbling over what felt like half a dozen responses.

George's eyes had a twinkle of amusement in them. "So where you going all dressed up?"

"Oh, he's bringing me to The Pier."

"Nice place. It's seafood, though."

"Ha… Silas made sure to mention that."

"He must be really into you. I can't wait to tell Annie. We've been a little worried about Silas. He's been single for a long time." George turned when the kitchen door opened and Nancy walked in. "Did you hear the good news?"

She stopped short, looked between us, and asked while handing over a ticket, "We've all won the lotto and get to retire in the Florida Keys?"

"Silas has a date," George corrected.

"Holy cow, *really*?" Nancy put her hands on her hips. "It's been a while. With who?"

George jutted a thumb at me.

"To be honest, I'm a bit disappointed it's not cash and the Keys too, Nancy," I stated.

She smirked. "Smartass. Silas is a real sweetheart. Congratulations!"

"This news is going to be spread all over town by the end of the day, isn't it?" I asked.

"It'll probably reach Whitefield too," she answered. Nancy pointed to the ticket she'd given George and then said, "McGrath's to-go order. He wants cheddar cheese in—"

"His tomato soup, I know," George finished.

"He gets mad if I don't repeat it," Nancy remarked, raising her hands overhead and walking back to the swinging door. "Like after ordering that soup three days a week for two years straight we'd forget his damn cheese."

George made a rumbling sound in his chest that I suspect was a suppressed chuckle. "Anyway, Silas also mentioned that burger."

"Did he pick the kimchi off?"

This time, George did laugh. "Would you believe that picky eater ate the whole damn thing? I said you'd get to come up with the special if he did, right? So what'll it be?"

We got to work on orders after that. There wasn't enough time to prep anything particularly extravagant for the Bridge crew who'd requested the day's special, so I settled on a dish an ex-boyfriend had taught me—his recipe for a creamy, spicy, baked macaroni and cheese being the only boon to a relationship that'd otherwise been a total waste of my time. It'd have probably hit the spot even more if it was cold and wintry, but really, any day was a good day for mac 'n' cheese.

"Ever driven in snow?" George asked as he stuffed a paper bag with the delivery orders.

"It snowed an inch while I was in Pasadena last year," I said.

George pushed the bag across the prep table toward me. "A whole inch, huh?"

"I'm a good driver, remember? There aren't moose in Pasadena. I did pass a car that'd crashed into a mailbox, though."

"Boyo, I can't wait until you experience your first Thanksgiving in New Hampshire."

I picked up the bag, holding the bottom with both hands. "Yeah?"

"It ain't called the Great White Mountains for nothing." At that, George waved me off.

It occurred to me, while driving to the Bridge for the now-habitual food drop-off and bullshitting with the guys, that both George and I had suggested—*assumed?*—I'd be in New Hampshire long enough to see the leaves change, to experience the first snowfall, and that I wouldn't be back in LA the very second I'd made enough cash to pay for my car repairs. That was the whole reason I was at Eatery to begin with, after all.

To fix my car.

Not because a small-town guy saw some sort of potential in me that no one else ever did.

Not because I made some mean tacos or could flip a patty or had hijacked a secret mac 'n' cheese family recipe for my own devices.

And *definitely* not because that same guy thought I was a decent match for his little brother, and said brother was about as pure as the driven snow.

Fuck.

And there I was—full circle—right back to snow.

New Hampshire just *wasn't* my vibe, though.

I mean, *right*? Because after I fixed my car, I'd head back to California, fresh and revitalized after my cross-country trip, and return to… well, not a job. No real friendships either, not even a dog. Christ on a goddamn spinning cracker in outer space. My future held actual opportunities for the first time in my adult life, and here I was trying to convince myself to plow back into the past. Because a future, even a positive one, was still uncertain, and at least I couldn't be disappointed by what had already transpired.

"This place is fancy," I said, my voice low.

Silas had gone home to change out of his manly-man flannel and Carhartt before picking me up for our date at The Pier. He cut quite a handsome figure in dark jeans and a button-down, but he also looked supremely uncomfortable—literally, not emotionally. His shoulders and pecs were about to Hulk out of the shirt. I figured that top had been purchased several hundred bench presses ago.

"So I noticed your car is now fixed," I continued.

Silas shifted and tugged at his collar.

"How much did it cost?"

"Don't worry about it."

"Don't *worry* about it?" I repeated. "Come on. One of the first things you said to me when we met was that I'd be getting your bill."

Silas shrugged, and the top button of his shirt looked ready to completely give up.

"Go ahead and undo that first one, dude," I said, motioning to my own shirt. "It might hit me in the eye if you move again."

It was hard to tell, with the lights down low and only having the flickering candle on our tabletop to go by, but I think Silas was blushing. He quickly undid the top button on his shirt and let out a held breath that sounded a hell of a lot like relief.

"So, not that I'm rolling in Benjamins, but why the about-face? *I* hit *your* car, remember?"

"I remember."

"Is this because we're on a date?"

Silas shook his head and fiddled with his salad fork. "Jack 'n' Jill's Autobody owed me a favor, so they took care of it at no charge."

"Really?"

"Yes."

"No, I mean, the place is called Jack 'n' Jill's?"

"Oh." Silas laughed under his breath. "Yes. That's their real names."

A waiter joined us after another moment. I tried to convince Silas to give raw oysters a try, but he adamantly shook his head and muttered something about having to maintain certain lines in the sand. I ordered them for myself as an appetizer and snapper for the main meal. Silas chose halibut, the mildest fish on the menu, I noted, but hey, he was trying for me. The waiter nodded, said a few "very good" and "excellent choices" before asking about wine. Silas shrugged, so I chose a pinot grigio on the cheaper side of the menu, and then the waiter left us.

"You sure you want wine?" I asked after a moment. "I bet they have whiskey at the bar," I continued, motioning to the far side of the restaurant.

"Wine is okay," Silas insisted with a tone of uncertainty. "You're supposed to pair it with seafood after all, right?"

"Right."

He nodded at that, and after a moment of silence, asked, "How're things with George?"

"Good. Great, actually. He's letting me choose and cook the specials going forward."

"Really?"

"I suspect at least until someone complains," I joked.

But Silas smiled so sweetly and so sincerely that it nearly broke my heart. "I can't imagine anyone would. Certainly not my crew." He picked up the salad fork again, staring at the tines while saying, "I loved that mac 'n' cheese."

"Even though it was spicy?"

He nodded. "You know… I was thinking… something you said last night."

"Oh God. I said *a lot* of things last night. I never shut up."

"About not doing anything right in LA."

I smacked my forehead. "I was a touch dramatic."

"I just mean—maybe your calling wasn't tattooing."

I arched a brow. "No shit."

"No, I—you're a food artist," Silas said, his voice quieting toward the end of the statement.

Our waiter returned to the table with the bottle of wine.

I leaned over the plates and cutlery and whispered, "Are you pulling my leg?"

"No, of course not," Silas answered.

The cork was popped and the waiter poured the white wine into our glasses before moving away.

"Really?"

"Maybe that's a stupid description—" Silas began.

I waved both hands, very nearly smacking the wine glass off the table. "No, no. It's… it's really nice, actually."

"You should ask George about a full-time cook position."

"I should?"

"I mean, if you enjoy it."

"I do," I quickly said. I picked up my glass and stared at the contents. "It's just funny you say that, because earlier today I was wondering if maybe I'd… stick around longer than I'd initially intended."

Silas picked up his own glass and held it out. "I would selfishly be very happy about that."

"What should we drink to?"

He was thoughtful before suggesting, "Moose."

"Oh my God." I laughed and tapped the rim of my glass against his. "To moose."

I'd hardly taken a sip of the pinot grigio before a fire alarm began wailing. I startled and spilled wine all over my lap. Cooks poured out from the kitchen doors—one of them shouting, "Grease fire!"—and then waitstaff were hastily ushering patrons out the front doors as smoke billowed from the hallway.

Silas moved around the table, took my hand, and led the way out to the parking lot. By the time we reached his car and turned back to the restaurant—a whole twenty seconds, tops—smoke was wafting up from the back of the building and sirens echoed from the opposite end of town.

"Fucking hell," I said.

"Come on." Silas opened the driver's door and motioned me to do the same. "We need to get out of here before the fire trucks box us in."

CHAPTER SIX

So our date ended up being Chinese takeout on the couch. Silas handed me one of the freshly microwaved containers, sat down beside me, then put an arm around my shoulders.

"I'm sorry about how the dated ended," I said before taking a bite of a greasy egg roll.

"You didn't start the fire."

"I was really looking forward to a classy night out."

"Do you have tomorrow off?"

"No… why?"

"Call George. Tell him I'm going to take you swimming."

"Swimming?"

"Yeah."

"It's April."

Silas moved his arm and shoveled pork fried rice onto a plastic fork dwarfed in his massive paw. "You only live once."

"Because you died from hypothermia." I finished the egg roll, stood, and asked, "Can I use your landline? My cell is spotty this far out."

Silas nodded and jutted a thumb toward the kitchen.

I walked around the couch, stepped over Ben, and went into the kitchen. Silas had a damn rotary phone mounted to the wall. I picked up the receiver. "What's his number?" I spun the dial as Silas called it out.

The other end clattered loudly as it was picked up, and then a little girl said, "Hi, Uncle Silas."

"Oh. Er—hi. This is Gideon Joy. Do you remember me? You hit me in the face with a door."

"Why is your number the same as my uncle's?"

"Uh…." Did she know her uncle liked boys? She must have. But I wasn't going to hurdle that fence blind. "Fuc—I mean, so weird, right? Hey, can I talk to your dad?"

"Hold on." She put the phone down and her voice retreated while calling for George.

"Silas?" George asked a moment later.

"Gideon," I corrected.

"Is everything okay?"

"Yeah, fine. As long as you're not asking about the date."

"What? Why? What's wrong?"

"Nothing with Silas," I hastily answered, lowering my voice while glancing around the corner. Said man was flipping through muted sports channels. "He's fine. Good. Hot. I mean—the restaurant had a grease fire."

"You're kidding."

"No."

"I'll be damned. Sorry to hear that."

"Anyway," I said before taking a deep breath, "Silas wanted me to ask if I could have tomorrow off. He wants to take me swimming." I peeked around the corner again before asking, "Is he trying to kill me?"

"I can hear you," Silas said from the living room.

George was laughing. "Sounds like he's going to the Rock."

"I'm assuming you don't mean Dwayne Johnson. So what's the Rock? Is it a technical term, like *the Bridge*?"

"Hey now."

"Sorry," I grumbled. "I've got a bug up my ass."

"You can have tomorrow off. It's no problem. Have fun swimming."

"Thanks."

"Good night, Gideon."

"Night." I hung up and returned to the living room. I plopped down beside Silas again, put my head on his shoulder, and said, "Day off obtained."

Silas patted my thigh and flipped to a basketball game. He set the remote aside and resumed picking around the peas in his rice. "Tomorrow is another day."

"I know."

"Don't be upset."

I sat up long enough to raise Silas's arm so that I could rest my head against his chest. "I'm not. You're right. We'll have fun tomorrow."

We ate our takeout, watched tall guys on Team A fight tall guys on Team B over a ball, and I eventually fell asleep to the rich silence of the woodland surrounding Silas's property and his quiet irritability over the game.

"I remember driving through here," I said, staring out the passenger window at the towering mountains on either side of the car. "Franconia Notch, right?"

"Just 'the Notch' works."

I glanced at Silas as he pulled the sun visor down when the bright morning rays hit the windshield. "You folks simplify everything, don't you?"

Silas shrugged. "There's only one notch. No need to be specific."

"I bet this road is a bitch in the snow," I said after a moment.

"Ever driven in snow?"

"George asked me that too. How hard can it be?"

Silas smiled to himself. "It snows about six months of the year up here."

"You don't think I can handle it?"

"I think you can do anything," he corrected without missing a beat. Silas pointed straight up as we rounded a corner. "That's where the Old Man used to be."

I looked out the passenger window again. "Whose old man?"

"It was a rock formation."

"That explains the New Hampshire state quarter."

Silas nodded.

"So what happened to it?"

"The freezing and thawing started to erode the cliffside in the '20s," Silas explained in his pleasant, gentle rumble of a voice. "Caretakers maintained it every summer, but it finally fell in 2003."

"You guys will have to put the fluffernutter sandwich on all these state signs now," I teased.

"I think those originated in Massachusetts."

"All right, smarty-pants." I reached over to pat Silas's thigh—good God, how many squats did he do for the man-of-steel physique?—and asked, "So where are we going?"

"It's a pond. George brought me swimming there when we were younger. There's a waterfall."

"Are there fish?"

"I guess so."

"Ew!"

Silas smiled and said, eyes still on the road, "You'll be fine."

"If something touches me," I said, "I'm going to scream so loud, it'll shatter glass."

"Fair enough."

I lifted up in my seat to tug at the wedgie my swim shorts were creating under my jeans. They'd been an early-morning purchase on our way out of town and weren't the best fit. "This is a date, right?"

"Sure."

"Take two?"

"Take two."

Only a moment of quiet passed between us before I said suddenly, "I should shit or get off the pot."

Silas looked at me. "Sorry?"

"I mean—I've always held myself back. From, like… everything. Because when something shitty happens, I'm afraid if I change my routine, it'll get even worse."

"You quit your job, though," Silas pointed out as he put on his blinker and made a right turn onto a dirt side road.

"But why stop there?" I asked. "I mean, what's keeping me from asking George for a full-time position? What's holding me back from asking if I can cook instead of bus?"

Silas slowed as loose pebbles pinged the underside of the car. "This is a rhetorical question?"

"Right, don't answer it."

He nodded.

"And what the hell is keeping me from staying if I *like* living here? Better yet, what's keeping us from being official instead of tap-dancing around a relationship?"

Silas pulled up to a clearing, parked beside a weather-worn picnic table under a massive pine tree, turned the car off, and looked at me.

"That last one wasn't rhetorical," I remarked.

"Oh, sorry."

I unbuckled my seat belt and leaned closer to Silas. "I like you."

"I like you too."

"And I think there's chemistry."

He smiled a little shyly, and it was fucking adorable. "I think so too."

"Want to be boyfriends?"

"Yes." Such a simple response, and yet there was a gravity encircling it—encircling Silas—encircling *us*.

I grabbed the back of his head and gave his mouth a firm kiss. "Cool," I whispered as I pulled back.

Silas rubbed my jawline with the pad of his thumb and then got out of the car. I climbed out after him, and we undressed in the shade of the tree.

"Just when I imagine you couldn't be hiding any more tattoos," he said, folding his T-shirt.

I shoved my jeans down and pointed at my pale thighs covered in bright ink. "Oh, I've got more."

Silas adjusted the swim trunks hanging dangerously low on his hips. "I'll have to count them sometime."

"I promise I don't have a dick or butthole tattoo. Although I know someone who does."

His eyes grew wide. "Which?"

"Both."

He snorted, shook his head, and once we'd both left our piles of clothes on the picnic table, he took my hand and led the way along a steep, overgrown foot trail. It was slow work in bare feet, but as we neared the top of what he said was a hill but I considered a small fucking mountain, the sound of a stream cut through the heavy canopy. We broke through the dense vegetation, and the temperature noticeably dropped as we walked along the bank.

"Uh, Silas? Where's this water runoff from?"

"The mountains."

"The mountains we passed that still had snow on the peaks?"

The sound of the water grew to a steady roar as Silas led the way toward a massive slab of stone—sorry, the Rock—overlooking the waterfall and pool below. Silas squeezed my hand, waded into the water, and dragged me with him.

I let out a very undignified shriek. "Holy shit. Holy shit. It's so cold. Silas, what the fuck!"

He helped me onto the boulder, a huge grin on his face as he looked over the edge. "Come on."

"Whoa, wait. No way. I am *not* jumping into an ice bath."

"It's exhilarating," Silas answered. He gently pried my hands free from his body. "Once-in-a-lifetime experience."

"No fucking way."

"Do it to say you did, Gideon." Silas leaned closer, kissed just to the side of my mouth, and then cannonballed off the ledge.

I leaned over and watched Silas's blurry form break the surface of the water, then he laughed loudly and wiped his hair from his face. "How're your balls?" I shouted.

"Cold," he called, treading water. "Come on. Don't be afraid."

I chafed my arms vigorously as the spray of freezing water caused my skin to pimple with gooseflesh. Who thought freezing their nads off was acceptable first—er—second date material? A mountain man who didn't date much, I guessed. But this was so dumb. I should go back to the trail, hike down, and meet Silas.

Shit or get off the pot.

The echo of my own epiphany rang louder than the falling water. Goddammit. I couldn't have had that come-to-Jesus moment after this? I lowered my arms to my sides and let out a breath. I *should* do what makes me happy.

Not that *this*, per se, was it, but Silas made me happy.

Taking a chance made me happy.

Not being an anxiety-ridden ball of fear and self-loathing made me happy.

And not being the best at something… maybe that made me happy too.

"Watch out!" I shouted before jumping off the Rock.

The water was so cold, it was like pins and needles pricking every square inch of my body at once. I shot up to the surface, coughing and sputtering and flailing. Silas put one hand on my waist and pulled me closer while treading water with the other. I wrapped my arms around his neck, pressed my chest to his, and proceeded to leech as much body heat as I could.

"Fun, right?" he asked.

"F-fun?" I repeated, teeth chattering. "You're c-crazy."

Silas began to swim backward, pulling my half-frozen corpse with him. "That California blood is thin."

"I feel attacked."

He chuckled and said as we splashed out of the pond, "We'll get you ready for a New England winter yet." Silas rubbed my biceps a few times before adding, "Let's go back to the car. I packed towels and snacks."

It was a quicker walk back to the isolated overlook coming from the pond than it was trekking up the hill and along the stream. But when we reached Silas's car and the sun-bleached table, I noticed—

"Where're our clothes?"

Silas let go of my hand and made a circuit around the table and tree. "Maybe someone came by."

"And stole our clothes?"

He shrugged. "Kids, maybe."

"Great. Just fucking great," I said, throwing my hands up. I walked to the car and yanked on the passenger door, but the handle snapped back.

Locked.

"Silas…." I looked over the roof at him. "Please tell me you have your keys."

He stared at me, then the car. "Why would I take car keys with me knowing I was going to jump off a waterfall?"

"Son of a bitch." I tugged the handle again in frustration as Silas started hunting through the tall grass. I got down on one knee and found my glasses under the car. I grabbed them, checked the lenses, then put them on. There was nothing else underneath, so I got to my feet and joined the search for our belongings.

It took the better part of the day before we'd found Silas's jeans—*up a tree*—his keys thankfully still in the pocket, at least. And when we finally left the Notch, we were cold, sunburned, bug-bit, and missing my socks, Silas's shirt, his left shoe, and my right.

"Good morning," George said from where he stood at the front counter of Eatery the next day. "How was—whoa."

I'd woken up in a shit mood. I wasn't mad at Silas or anything, just deeply, *deeply* annoyed that once again our date had been ruined by outside forces. I knew my luck was hilariously pathetic, but come the hell on—first a grease fire and now this? What was going to happen—*nope*. Never mind. I wasn't even going to put a suggestion out there for Miss Karma to overhear.

"We got punk'd," I said to George. I scratched at my chest, which had been eaten alive by some fucking pest Silas called a 'no-see-um' and he wasn't even kidding. "Someone stole our clothes and hid them up a tree."

George's eyebrows shot up. "Huh."

"I know." I stopped at the counter, put my elbows on it, and huffed. "Hey."

"Hey, back."

"I want to cook."

"Well, you need to pick today's special—"

"No, I mean, full-time. I want to be a chef."

George folded his massive arms across his chest. He looked very much like Silas then, and I couldn't believe I'd never put two and two together on my own. "Is that so?"

"It's so."

"How long you thinking of staying in New Hampshire?"

"Foreseeable future."

"And where are you planning to stay?"

"Er… well, Silas—"

"Said you could stay with him?" George finished.

"Please don't be the bully big brother."

George laughed. He reached across the counter and clapped my shoulder roughly. "Welcome to Lancaster, boyo."

Even though it was finally looking as if I was getting my life together—what with the job, boyfriend, blossoming friendships with locals who'd taken me in as one of their own without question—hell, I now had enough cash to put my car in the shop too—there was still one aspect I was failing at with absolute flying colors.

The date.

Third time had not been the charm for us.

Nor the fourth.

Or even the fifth.

Silas had wanted to take our relationship slow, and he was so charmingly old-fashioned in that respect, it *really* did mean no sex. Like, not even hot-and-heavy petting. He wanted us to spend real time together and learn more about each other. And I dug it. I mean, who wouldn't enjoy simplistic dates like a classic black-and-white film, shopping at a farmers' market, or even fishing? Except that the projector broke five minutes into the movie we'd traveled two hours to go see. The market got washed out by an unexpected downpour. And I successfully managed to get stuck with a rusty fishhook and spent the afternoon at the hospital instead of learning how to cast.

At this point it wasn't even about the sex. I mean, yeah, Silas was totally a hunk of man I'd go down on faster than you could snap at, but I just wanted one date that didn't end in Band-Aids and tears.

Just one.

So I'd stop feeling like a sack of shit weighing him down. Because while I was coming to terms with being average and that average was, in fact, an acceptable goal in life, Silas deserved a *great* boyfriend. And if I couldn't be that—the best where it actually mattered—then I had no right to keep dating him.

"You're not cursed," Silas said as he parked his car in front of George's house and climbed out from behind the wheel.

"That's easy for you to say," I answered, following. "If I step foot onto George's property, a goddamn sinkhole will probably open up underneath his house."

"Now you're being dramatic." Silas walked around the front of the car, reached out, and placed his hand on the back of my neck. "This isn't a date. It's dinner with my brother's family. Deep breath."

I hadn't met Annie, George's wife, yet. Between her schedule as a hospital nurse, George's at Eatery, and the comings and goings of their young and wild child, the entire family hadn't had a day off all month that included having enough energy leftover for guests.

And I just knew, because I was *me*, I'd do something to completely humiliate myself in front of her and then she'd spend her evening badgering George for hiring a total dunce, and then George would grow to resent me, and then Silas would become frustrated and—

Silas squeezed the back of my neck. "Are you panicking?"

"A little."

He leaned down and kissed me. "It'll be all right."

"Uncle Silas!"

Silas turned to the front door and smiled. He crouched, swept Ellen off her feet, and spun her overhead. "Hi, Ellie. Have you been good?"

She nodded and wrapped her little arms around his neck. "GJ," she stated upon meeting my gaze.

I laughed at that nickname. "Yeah. What's up, Ellen?"

"My mom said you're dating Uncle Silas like Megan is dating Uncle Ryan, but that I'm not supposed to call you uncle yet, like I don't call Megan auntie yet," she explained in one rapid breath, like she'd been prompted a few times to remember this.

Silas looked at me, that cute blush of his back for the world to see. "Annie's brother Ryan and his girlfriend."

"Ah. Got it." I looked at Ellen and shrugged my shoulders. "You can call me whatever you want. I don't mind."

"Uncle GJ," she answered, her expression scary serious.

"Uh, sure," I said, nodding.

Ellen smirked suddenly and then wriggled free from Silas's arms. "Mom and Dad are in the backyard. Come on!" She took his hand and dragged Silas around the side of the house.

I followed close behind into a huge backyard. It'd been cleared for flowerbeds and bushes, a swing set for Ellen and a barbeque area for the parents, and even a tidy little garden to the far left, ready for seedlings to sprout at any time. The property was completely surrounded by towering birches and pines, and the cool breeze, rustling leaves, and bird songs sort of brought me back to early morning at the Bartholomews, and it calmed me a little.

A woman with blonde hair in a ponytail was standing beside George at the grill. She laughed at something he said, shoved him, and then swatted at him with a bottle opener when George jabbed back with a spatula. He noticed us over her shoulder and called out in greeting.

Annie trotted toward us and said with a big smile, "You must be Gideon Joy. It's nice to finally meet you." She held a hand out.

I shook it and said, "Likewise. George talks about you all the time."

"Aww, does he? He talks about you all the time," she countered before winking. Annie gave Silas a hug next. "These big Bright boys act all stoic, but they're nothing but gooey on the inside."

Silas awkwardly smiled and seemed more than happy when Ellen began tugging his arm and asking him to push her on the swings. "Sure, okay, sweetie," he answered.

Annie inclined her head toward the grill, table, and an ice chest. "Want a beer, Gideon?"

"Yes, please," I answered quickly. "One for both hands." I followed her across the lawn, where she nabbed a bottle, popped the top, and handed it over. "Thanks." I took a swig, sighed, and then inhaled the aroma of burgers and hot dogs a few feet away.

"Bad day?" she asked.

"No. I mean, I'm just sort of nervous."

"Yeah, I've heard about all the dates," she replied.

"Who hasn't?" I grumbled.

Annie smiled and opened a beer for herself. "I've known Silas for a decade. The man has more patience than a saint. He'd go on a million dates with you."

I picked at the label on the bottle with my thumbnail. "I guess so."

"Want to hear something that'll make you feel better?"

I let out a ghost of a laugh and looked up. "Sure. Hit me."

"First night of our honeymoon," Annie began, tilting the head of her bottle in George's direction, "he slipped and fell getting out of the resort pool and broke his leg. We tried for a makeup honeymoon the next year—cruise ship. I had food poisoning the entire trip."

"Jesus."

Annie nodded. "Sometimes you just have to laugh it off."

It seemed simple, right? Laugh off the wacky bullshit and move on with my life. But Annie didn't have the bad luck I had. She didn't feel like the only chance she had to breathe was to run across the entire country. She didn't feel the way my gut would clench up before something terrible inevitably happened.

Terrible like—like Saint Silas finding his breaking point with me.

"Oh shit. I forgot the potato salad," Annie said, looking at the table. "I'll be right back." She headed toward the home's back door.

I walked to the grill and joined George. "Hey. Need another beer?"

"I'm good here," George answered, holding up a half-full bottle. "How're you two doing?"

"Good," I lied. I watched Silas push Ellen, who was screaming in delight as her swing obtained some serious air.

"He's a great uncle," George stated, having turned to watch as well. "Always thought he'd be a daddy by now."

"Why isn't he?"

George returned to the grill and flipped a few burgers. "I think, when he was younger, he was concerned about being gay in a small town and trying to raise a kid. But people around here, they're mostly good. Everyone loves Silas."

"Resident good boy," I answered.

George laughed. "That's right. He dated a guy a while back who had a kid, but it didn't work out." George grabbed a plate and started picking up the hot dogs with a pair of tongs. "Not because of the kid, I mean. I think now he just wants to focus on having a partner."

"He sure isn't getting a family out of me."

"Adoption is—"

"No, I mean… who would trust me with a kid? How many times a week do you hear a crash and bang followed by me cussing and Nancy asking for the first-aid kit?"

"A little bad luck doesn't mean you can't have a family." George pointed the tongs at me. "If you want one, that is. If not…." He glanced at Silas a final time. "Pretty sure he'd still be over the moon for you."

I hadn't slept well that night. I told Silas it was the hot dogs and not a big deal, but in all sincerity, it *was* a big deal. I was fucking freaking out. Annie thought she was helping by sharing her honeymoon snafus with me, and sure, they sucked. Breaking your leg on your honey *totally sucked*. But she and George *made it* to their honeymoon. Silas and I couldn't even finish a date. Coupled with the knowledge that apparently Silas would be very happy to settle down with a family of his own and I couldn't even find my ass with a flashlight on a good day? Why was he wasting his time with a loser like me?

That thought hurt all the more as I lay in bed with Silas. His big body was pressed against my back, one strong arm thrown over me. It felt so good to be held like this—it felt like safety and hope and love—but I didn't deserve it. I could swallow being an average cook, living an average life in an average town. That was okay, honestly. But I *couldn't* be average to Silas.

And I knew average, at this point, was a compliment.

I slipped free from bed without waking him, tiptoed around Ben on the floor, got dressed, and left the house for some alone time. George was still letting me use the Eatery delivery car, so I slid in behind the wheel, backed out of the driveway, and left Union Road. I drove through the itty-bitty heart of Dalton with the window rolled down, listening to the wind cut across the angles of the car and the last of the peepers sing their Barry Manilow love songs before the sun rose. I followed the main road with the Connecticut River (I finally remembered to google it the other week) hugging one side, before coming to a stop at the T in the road. Right would take me to Lancaster and left would take me over Silas's freshly restored covered bridge and into Vermont.

I pulled onto the side of the road, parked, got out, and walked across the empty stretch of asphalt. It was dark inside the bridge. My steps echoed off the old beams underfoot and overhead, making it sound like an entire army of Hot Mess Gideon Joys were taking a panic stroll at five o'clock in the morning. I stopped at about the midpoint, put my face to the wall, and studied the water below. It was so calm, the surface looked like glass.

I stayed there for a while, lost in thought and not even noticing when the frogs stopped peeping and the birds started singing and someone was calling my name. I jerked and looked toward the New Hampshire end of the bridge to see a big form backlit by the sun.

"Silas?"

"*Gideon*." Silas ran into the bridge. "I woke up and you were gone. You left your phone, no note, and when I saw your car—I thought something happened to you," he continued, his voice bordering on honest-to-God upset.

"I'm sorry," I said, looking up at Silas as he came to a stop in front of me. I took off my glasses long enough to hastily wipe my eyes with the back of my hand. "Sorry," I repeated. "I needed to get away and think."

"Think about what?" Silas put his huge paws on my shoulders.

His weight was my foundation to the here and now, a reminder that my failures and shortcomings had gone nowhere over the last hour, and then I was bawling like a baby.

"Everything," I sobbed.

"Oh my God, Gideon. Please don't cry. I'm so sorry. I didn't—"

"You didn't do anything wrong, Mountain Man," I said between hiccups. "*I* did."

"What did you do?"

"I've screwed everything up, just like LA."

Silas moved his hands up to cup my face. "How?"

I opened my mouth, shut it, then tried again, but with everything balanced on the tip of my tongue, I realized how stupid it sounded, and I was mortified to vocalize it all in front of the audience I cared most about.

"See?" he said, smiling. "It's not true."

"It is so."

Silas shook his head while wiping my cheeks with his thumbs. "Do you like working at Eatery?"

"I love it."

"Do you like living in New Hampshire?"

"A lot."

"Do you like me?"

I swallowed the baseball-sized lump in my throat. "More than sex, whiskey, and puppy-dog kisses."

"Then how have you screwed anything up?" Before I could answer, he added, "Is this because of the dates?"

My eyes started to well up again, and I nodded.

"Gideon…." Silas pulled me to his chest and nearly snapped me in two, his hug was so strong. "I'm not looking for glitz and action. I want to spend my life with someone who is quietly content with theirs."

"I-I am. I really am."

"Then why do you keep beating yourself up about dates? I don't need to go on an adventure to enjoy spending time with you."

I had to give Silas a push before he realized how tightly he was holding on, apologized, and let go. "What kind of boyfriend am I, though?" I asked, fixing my glasses. "Not once have we finished a date that didn't end in a flat tire or a rolled ankle or—fuck me, what about the bear?"

Silas smiled. "You're a boyfriend who makes me happier than I've ever been, who will likely never live a dull life, and will always have a story to share because of it."

I looked down at my back-up pair of Chucks, since we never did find the second shoe after the swimming incident. These were so worn-out, I'd actually wrapped duct tape around the toe to keep the sole from falling off. "What about having a family? What if I'm not cut out for that?"

"A family is whatever you make it to be. If that means you, me, and the dog, that's okay. If it means… more… that's okay too. We can only live *today*, Gideon. Don't worry about tomorrow before it's even happened." Silas tilted my head back and kissed my forehead.

I took a deep breath and stared up at him. "I think I have an idea for a date I can't set on fire."

Silas seemed dubious but warily asked, "What?"

"We stay home. Sit outside. And look at the stars."

So we did.

And it probably sounds corny, but when I finally accepted that being Gideon Joy meant I'd always be an accident-prone dumbass who managed to somehow worm his way into the hearts of folks willing to hold back a chuckle when I found the one fresh dog turd to step in and then spent ten minutes trying to dig it out of my shoe treads, life sort of managed to fall into place.

Having bad luck didn't mean happiness was unobtainable.

For me, it just meant happiness had been hiding in the White Mountains of northern New Hampshire and a moose had to show me the way.

Under the stars that night—I experienced joy.

Please continue reading for the additional short story, *Kneading You* (A Lancaster Story: Book One), available as an exclusive paperback bonus!

Kneading You
A LANCASTER STORY
C.S. POE

This is a work of fiction. Names, characters, places, and incidents either are the product of the author's imagination or are used fictitiously, and any resemblance to actual persons, living or dead, business establishments, events, or locales is entirely coincidental.

Kneading You
Copyright © 2016, 2019, 2020 by C.S. Poe

All rights reserved. No part of this book may be reproduced in any form, stored in any retrieval system, or transmitted in any form by any means—electronic, mechanical, photocopy, recording, or otherwise—without prior written permission of the publisher, except as provided by United States of America copyright law. For permission requests and all other inquiries, contact: contact@cspoe.com

Published by Emporium Press
https://www.cspoe.com
contact@cspoe.com

Cover Art by Reese Dante
Cover content is for illustrative purposes only and any person depicted on the cover is a model.

Published 2020.
First Edition published 2016. Second Edition 2019. Third Edition 2020.
Printed in the United States of America

Digital eBook ISBN: 978-1-952133-12-1

AUTHOR'S NOTE

While each book in A Lancaster Story can be read as a standalone, occasional crossover of characters does occur. Check out each title in the series to fully enjoy all of the residents of Lancaster, New Hampshire.

CHAPTER ONE

I rushed up the slippery steps of Lancaster's old library to greet the portly man awaiting me. "I'm sorry I'm late." I held a hand out. "Christopher Hughes. It's a pleasure."

"Logan Fields," the man said, shaking with an unnecessarily firm grip. "I'm on the town's Board of Selectmen. I'm in charge of overseeing our library crisis. Come on inside." He turned around, used an old skeleton key to unlock the front door, and led the way into the dim interior.

I had recently moved to the charming town of Lancaster, New Hampshire. No more than ten years ago, they'd outgrown the title of village—everyone was very proud, I was told. I'd spent most of my life in suburbs in the more populated, southern portion of the state. And while it was nice and convenient, I'd always dreamed of living in a small community where folks all knew one another and there was a real sense of closeness.

I'd certainly found it here.

But not a job.

That was a rather elusive beast.

But such was the way of life in these tiny blips on the map. There were not a lot of job openings on a consistent basis, and so far my options were part-time clerk at the gas station, part-time bagger at the grocery store, or nada. Although I had a college degree, studies in nineteenth-century literature didn't get you far in a town that required more practical services. I'd been ready to become a bagger too, if it meant paying the rent on time. But then I heard about *this*.

The library.

Lancaster was in a panic after their librarian—a nice old lady who I swear must have been older than the building itself—passed away, and they needed someone to take over.

Ding, ding, ding! Christopher Hughes, come on down. You've won a cozy little position in an antique library. How do you feel?

I can afford dinner now—I feel great!

Logan Fields flicked on an old light switch as I shut out the winter day behind us. "Here she is. Pretty old place, isn't it?"

It was indeed. The library was small, nothing like I was used to. It was maybe the size of the downstairs of a large house. The woodwork was dark and rich, there were high ceilings, and gorgeous old moldings. I turned, whistling quietly as I took it all in. There was a desk for checkout closer to the wall—with no computer, I noted. An alcove stood just beyond that, completely stuffed with books. To the right of the main area was a closed door, and to the left was the study room—a long table with chairs situated in the middle. Bank lamps with green shades sat positioned on the tabletop, and some old leather-bound books and maps made the space look especially cozy.

"This is wonderful," I said.

Logan nodded. "Our public library has been open for over a hundred and fifty years. It's been here through thick and thin, and provided for people when they otherwise couldn't afford to learn." He turned to look down at me. "You must understand, a lot of folks up here—they don't have big-paying jobs like in the cities. They live paycheck to paycheck. My kids all came here, growing up." He looked pained. "This place means a lot to us all."

My hands were sweaty in my coat pockets. It felt like I needed to say something, assure him I was capable of the job, if he wanted to hire me, but I kept quiet.

Logan cleared his throat and patted his belly absently. "Anyway. Our old librarian passed on, as you know, and we need help. The state is looking to pull the funding from this facility."

"What?" I blurted. "*Why?*"

"Money. It's always about money. Why give a dinky little town like ours resources when they can better pump it into cities where they get more bang for their buck?" Logan huffed. "We need this place spruced up. Show them how vital this library is to the community. If we can show them how much use this place gets…."

"Do you not have that sort of information on file?"

Logan gave me a sheepish expression. "To be honest, the job doesn't pay much, and Beatrice held the position for eons. She didn't know how to use computers. So all that information is written by hand in her ledgers."

"Ah… okay."

Logan hurried to a nearby shelf, chose a book at random, and brought it back to me. "See, we don't have any sort of bar code system for checkout." He opened to the front page, where there was an old-fashioned library card in the pocket glued to the cover, with handwritten names and dates going as far back as 1947.

"Holy shit," I whispered.

Logan snorted. "Right." He shut the book and stared at me again. "What I'm asking of you might not be possible. I've got no budget for new books or supplies, and I've nothing to offer you in terms of support. Your job may very well be short-lived… but we need help. Plus, you've got that English degree—"

I waved my hands. "I don't have a degree in library science. I mean, I had a part-time job at my college library, but my degree is in *literature*. Oscar Wilde, Edgar Allan Poe, Mary Shelley—"

"That's no matter. None of the librarians in neighboring towns have an MLS either. We're very small. We don't necessarily need that sort of credential."

I looked around. The building was silent but alive. Over a hundred years of people passing through the arched doorway, of learning and studying. I felt a deep force tugging me to the available position, despite the lack of job security. It was strange. And not smart.

"I'll do it," I answered.

"You will?" Logan asked.

"Yes."

"*Thank you*," Logan said, grabbing both my hands in a vise lock and shaking hard. "Look. This room here"—he pointed at the closed door—"Beatrice shut it down after it came into disrepair, and she stuffed all those books into other places or the storeroom upstairs, beside the kitchenette." He reached into his wallet and fussed about for a moment before drawing out a business card. "This is the number to our local handyman. This guy always gives me a break on cost, and he'll fix that room up in a jiffy."

"Sure. I'll call him today," I said, taking the card.

"You have my number?" Logan asked.

I nodded. "Yes, sir."

"Good." He handed me the ring of skeleton keys.

"Wait, Mr. Fields," I said as he started to turn away. "How much time? Until the state decides whether to pull funding or not?"

"About a month."

"Oh."

Logan smiled, looking like a man brought back from the brink of death. "Godspeed to you, Christopher." He saw himself out.

I stood in the middle of the library, listening to the nothingness. I unbuttoned my jacket after a moment and tossed it and my scarf over the back of the chair at the checkout desk. If I had so little time to put this place into working order again, and maintain my job as a result, there wasn't a moment to waste. I didn't have anywhere else to be, right? I picked up the landline phone and dialed the number on the card.

It rang a few times before a deep voice answered. "Hello?"

"Uhm, hi, is this—" I looked at the card. "—Miles Sakasai?"

"This is," he confirmed.

"Good. My name is Christopher Hughes. Mr. Fields from the Board of Selectmen gave me your number."

Silence.

"So… I've been hired to take over the library and was told to call you for repairs."

"What do you need done?"

Excellent question. I moved around the desk, the phone cord stretching as I walked to the closed door. I tried the knob, but it was locked, so I sifted through my newly acquired keys.

"Mr. Fields said there was a room that was closed off." I paused to shove the door open with my shoulder once I got it unlocked. The room was dark and smelled of dust and *oldness*. I coughed loudly and waved a hand. "Shit."

"Are you okay?"

"Yeah, sorry," I replied. "I just got the door open. It looks like a lot of the shelves built into the bookcases along the walls are broken."

"Are you going to be at the library all day?" Miles's voice was a little rough-sounding. Gritty. I liked it a lot.

"Yeah, I'll probably be here day and night, by the looks of the place."

"I have no other jobs today. I'll be over soon." He hung up without another word.

I removed the receiver from my ear and stared at it. "All right, then." I shut the door so the odor wouldn't permeate the rest of the downstairs, and walked back to the desk to set the phone down.

There was a staircase near the study room that was roped off, but I pulled it aside and went up. The stairs creaked and groaned loudly with their age, disrupting the beautiful stillness of the library below. I reached the second-floor landing and flipped a light switch on the wall. To the left was a tiny, open space turned into a break room. It had a minifridge, sink, two cupboards, and an old table with mismatched chairs.

The next room was the bathroom, where I paused to wash some of the dust from my hands. The mirror was old and tarnished with black spots, but the reflection was that of a happy man in his late twenties. Definitely happy against all odds. Something in my gut told me this was my small-town calling. Plus, to be surrounded by books all day?

Heaven.

Pure bliss!

At least I had a basic understanding of library mechanics to rely on from my work-study job. Hopefully it'd be enough for me to get the ball rolling. And if this turned into a permanent position, maybe I could take some official classes on managing a library.

But one step at a time.

I patted down my sandy brown hair, which had been disheveled by the wind, and straightened the knot of my tie. I thought I looked pretty snazzy. I'd dressed professionally to meet Mr. Fields because I'd expected to be attending an actual interview. I hadn't thought I'd be handed the keys to the castle then and there. I wore dark checkered slacks and a black sweater-vest over a white shirt. The new black-framed glasses, which was pretty much what the last of my cash was spent on, gave me the stereotypical, nerdy appearance I'd always wanted for myself.

I finished in the bathroom, found the storeroom Mr. Fields had mentioned, and the boxes and boxes and *boxes* of books Beatrice had left in there. After a short time of surveying the mess, I realized there was no system in place for what was packed where. Children's books were mixed in with romance, mixed in with biographies. I ended up on the floor, sifting through boxes and making piles for at least a half an hour, before I heard the heavy door open and close downstairs.

"Hello?" someone called, his muffled voice drifting upstairs.

"Crap." I hastily got to my feet, my back protesting after being hunched over. "Coming! I'll be right there," I called, shutting the door and running to the staircase. I sounded like a stampede of kindergarteners coming down the old steps.

A man stood in the middle of the front room, looking toward the staircase. He was holding a heavy-looking toolbox in one hand while absently unbuttoning his coat with the other.

Miles Sakasai, I presumed.

And then I took him in for an extra second, because even though I hadn't moved here with the intention of settling down with a handsome country boy—well, not right away, at least—there was no way to deny he was *extremely* easy on the eye. Miles was a good head taller than me, and was probably a few years older. He had dark hair that was a little messy, like he'd just removed a winter hat prior to coming inside. He had the strong, wiry build of a man comfortable with and accustomed to manual labor.

Miles shifted his weight from one foot to the other. "Mr. Hughes?" he asked, his tone soft but voice so deep, it seemed to reverberate off the walls.

"Christopher," I corrected, reaching a hand out.

"You can call me Miles," he said, shaking.

"It's nice to meet you. Thank you for being able to come out right away."

He nodded, set his tool kit down, slid the backpack from his shoulder, and removed his coat. He had on a black T-shirt that showed off toned arms and a built chest. A number of bold and brightly colored tattoos on Miles's arms caught my gaze.

I had to admit, I totally crushed on guys with ink.

When Miles spoke, he said, "I'm a professional, I promise."

My head snapped up. "What? Sorry."

"The tattoos."

"Oh, I—"

"They make some folks uncomfortable. Older generation, usually."

Good job. You've offended the guy.

I felt heat rise from my neck and up to my cheeks. "N-no, I'm sorry. It's—they're fine, really."

Don't creep on him. Not until after the bookshelves are fixed.

Miles relaxed, if only slightly.

Before I could avoid not listening to my own advice, I bolted to the closed door and opened it for him. "So here's what the room looks like."

Miles cocked his head to glance through the doorway before walking to the checkout desk first. He set his coat and backpack neatly on top and took his tool kit to the room with him. He waved a hand in front of his face.

"I can open a window, if you don't mind being a bit cold," I offered.

"Please."

I sidestepped some collapsed shelving and went across the decent-sized room. I unlocked a big window, pushed and shoved, but the window didn't budge. "The hell? Is this nailed shut?"

"These old buildings," Miles said as he put his tool kit down and joined me. "Some have windows that have never been updated." He pointed to the thick rope that slid the window up and down. "See? You just need to give it an extra nudge." Miles shoved the window hard, and with a protesting groan, it went up.

"Ah-ha." I nodded, glancing up at him. "Thanks."

Miles offered a small, somewhat shy smile. "I'll try not to make too much noise."

"Don't worry about it. The library isn't open to the public right now." The dust still hung heavy in the air, and I coughed.

Miles put a hand on my upper back and turned me firmly toward the doorway. "You don't want to stay in here."

"Is there anything I can get you?" I asked while exiting.

"No."

"Sure?"

"Yes."

No small talk, got it.

I turned and offered Miles one last look. He stood patiently in the middle of the room, waiting for me to leave. "Well—uh, if you need me, I'm around."

CHAPTER TWO

My stomach growled and interrupted my destruction of the upstairs storeroom. I checked my watch and realized it was past one in the afternoon. I'd been upstairs for hours and was hungry as hell. Leaving my mess—I mean, the sorted piles—I went downstairs. The door to the side room was closed. I could hear Miles hammering away through the heavy wooden barrier.

I sat down at the checkout desk and found a folder with a handful of take-out menus stored inside. I sifted through them, my options mostly limited to pizza or Chinese, both of which I really didn't want. I needed to keep working after this, not take a food-induced coma nap. I was hemming and hawing over ordering a cheap sandwich from some place called Eatery when there was a knock at the front door. Before I could stand, it was opened, and a handsome man in a suit with an open coat walked in.

"You must be Christopher Hughes," he said with a wide grin and booming voice.

"Ah, yes, that's right." I stood and moved to shake the stranger's hand.

"Sam Bloom. I'm on the Board of Selectmen."

"Oh! It's a pleasure to meet you," I said, perking up.

"I see that Logan is already working you like a horse."

"It's not so bad. I'm enjoying it so far, and I've already got repairs underway."

"Uh-huh." Sam looked briefly toward the closed door. "So. If you have some time to spare, Christopher, I'd like to speak with you in private." He flashed me another smile, and I had to admit, I wasn't usually attracted to silver foxes, but Sam was smokin'. "Let's get some lunch—what do you say?"

I was pretty committed to that five-dollar sandwich, plus I wanted to keep working, but at the same time, I didn't want to upset the Board, who were essentially my new bosses. I hadn't gotten much further than "Er—well—" before Miles stepped out of the side room.

As soon as he and Sam made eye contact with each other, I swear the temperature in the building dropped to *frigid*. Miles pulled the bandana tied around his mouth down to his neck and wiped his dirty hands on his work jeans. Sam cleared his throat and straightened his posture.

"I see you're still working for peanuts, Miles," Sam said.

Miles didn't seem particularly agitated by the comment. "You set the budget," he replied calmly. He shut the door and walked to the stairs. "I'll be back in a moment," he said, his voice partially drowned out by the creaking steps.

I had turned to watch Miles before Sam put a hand on my arm. I glanced at him and Sam politely smiled.

"Sorry about that," he said. "Everyone knows one another's business around here." I wasn't entirely sure what he was implying, but I didn't get a chance to inquire, as Sam continued speaking. "Let me be frank, Christopher. This building won't survive."

"But Mr. Fields said—"

"It doesn't matter what Logan told you," Sam replied. "The state isn't going to pay for this place to remain open, and we cannot assume we'll receive enough grants every year to not need the state."

"But how can a community *not* have a library?" I asked, and maybe I sounded naïve, but that was like a town not having firefighters or police.

In my humble opinion, at least.

Sam smiled again, but this time it didn't feel entirely trustworthy. It was difficult to explain, but you know that gut instinct that tells you whether or not to trust a person? Almost like a fight-or-flight response? It was kicking in and saying something wasn't right about Mr. Bloom.

"I have a proposal for this property," Sam continued. "We need to stop clinging to the past. It's holding us back from becoming a town firmly rooted in the twenty-first century."

"What sort of proposal?" I asked warily.

"There are pockets of land here and there that cell phones get no service in. Some residents still rely on dial-up internet, believe it or not. I've proposed purchasing this property and the surrounding lots from the town to build a cell tower and a new shopping center. It'll create several new jobs and bring some life back to Main Street."

"How will you build a cell tower around the library?"

Sam laughed heartily, like I was dense. "You're a sweet guy, Christopher."

"I am?"

"We'd bulldoze the building. It's too old and needs too much work. It's not worth keeping."

"I—but—that's exactly why it *should* be kept. It's a landmark. There's so much history—"

"Yes, I know about the history. You sound like a mini-Logan. This library is not cost-effective. It's really that simple."

"But it's not about making money," I declared. "It's about having a safe and free place for people to come and learn. This town doesn't even have a bookstore—you have to drive nearly twenty miles to the closest one, and then you have to buy the book. Libraries are here for those who can't afford to make that purchase. For kids who need resources for school, or even—if we were able to purchase a computer or two, we'd have high-speed internet for those who need something better than dial-up. Libraries are crucial."

Sam was not smiling anymore. "I wanted to offer you a job, Christopher."

"I don't *want* to work at a shopping center," I replied firmly, crossing my arms. "I want to work here. I cannot in good faith step aside and see this place torn down."

Sam was quiet for a beat, like he was deciding on what to say next, but the creaking of Miles on the stairs kept him from offering further rebuttal. "I'm sorry to hear that. It's a shame you'll soon be unemployed." He turned to the front door. "Nice to meet you," he added, before walking out.

"Asshole," I muttered as the door slammed shut.

"He's insufferable," Miles stated.

I turned around to look at him standing on the last stair. "Did you hear what he said?"

Miles nodded. "Sam has made it no secret that he intends to purchase this land. He owns a small construction company, you see."

I shook my head, arms dropping to my sides. "I don't understand people like that. I know this place doesn't get the traffic a city library would, but…."

"It's still important," Miles finished. "I spent most of my childhood here."

"Really?"

He nodded again.

My stomach growled suddenly, loud enough to be mistaken for a monster in some underground cavern. "Oh God," I said, laughing and rubbing my stomach. "I was going to order food before that jerk came in."

"I brought lunch," Miles stated. "Enough to share."

"No, that's not necessary."

"It's better than most places in town." Miles fetched his backpack from the checkout desk.

I awkwardly joined his side. "That's really kind of you. Lunch will be on me next."

Miles removed a big thermos from the bag. "Just promise you won't order the chicken wings from Paul's Pizza."

"Why?"

"They aren't chicken."

I made a face and he laughed. He had a gorgeous laugh—deep and rich—and it made my entire body thrum with delight.

Miles unscrewed the top of the thermos, the lid doubling as a big cup which he poured a still-hot, creamy soup into. He passed it over and then pulled out a thick slice of bread, unwrapped it, and carefully tore it into two pieces.

I thanked him again, taking the offering. The bread was warm from being kept next to the thermos, had a golden crust, and a soft center. I took a small bite to taste. It was a simple white bread.

Or rather, a *delicious* white bread, I should say, bursting with flavor and tasting of everything precious and beautiful about the countryside. It reminded me of autumn leaves and crisp air. Of woodsmoke from log cabins and snowshoeing in winter. Of rustic home cooking and country fairs.

"Oh my God," I said before taking another bite.

Miles paused, holding a chunk of bread in his soup to sop up. "Is it no good?" he asked with concern.

"This… did you make this?" I asked, waving the bread.

"Yes," he said with clear hesitation.

"This is the best damn bread I've ever tasted."

Miles looked relieved, smiled a little, and said, "Thank you."

"My mom had a bread machine, but she never used it when I was growing up," I continued, tearing another piece free. I was sure the soup was homemade and delicious too, but this bread was *insane*. I could eat it all totally plain.

"I don't use a machine," Miles stated.

"No? Then how do you make it?"

He was starting to look more comfortable, like this topic was solid ground to stand on. I didn't think he was a reclusive guy, just shy. "By putting yeast in water, kneading it, letting it rise, punching it—"

"You get violent with the bread?"

Miles grinned. "To get the air out. Rise it some more, bake it, let it cool…."

"Wow. I don't think I've met someone who makes bread from scratch."

"It's relaxing."

"How long does it take?"

"Three or four hours."

"I'm eating four hours of effort?" I exclaimed. I looked at it again. "It's really good. Do you make any other kinds?"

"Yes."

"Like what?"

"Every kind. Oatmeal, wheat, raisin, cornmeal, sourdough, rye, herb—" Miles abruptly stopped. "You get the point."

"So," I said, dipping the bread into the soup and tasting the combination. "You bake and you fix broken things?"

Miles shrugged. "Pretty much. What about you?"

"I burn toast and once broke my finger with a hammer."

I lived in a little apartment on Water Street, above the local bank. One day I wanted to buy one of the Victorian houses that Lancaster was famous for, but considering I had only just become employed today, it'd probably be a while. I shut the door and flicked on the light switch before dropping my jacket and kicking off my shoes. I'd dragged home several of the heavy ledgers Beatrice kept records of every random bit of information in. I was going to spend the evening trying to glean some figures regarding spending, or inventory, or foot traffic—or *anything*, really.

I paused in the hall long enough to turn up the thermostat before going to the kitchen. I put the heavy books down on the table, then took a moment to make some hot chocolate.

"Spike it?" I asked myself, looking at the few bottles of liquor in the cupboard above the fridge.

Does a bear shit in the woods?

I poured a dash of marshmallow vodka into the mug and sat down with it.

All right, time to focus. Miles had successfully helped me forget a lot about my meeting with Selectman Sam, but now that he was nowhere in sight and I was left to my own devices, that unfortunate conversation came rushing back.

Sam Bloom was going to do everything he could to tear that building down. I mean, even if the library *was* shut down, it could always be transformed into something else. Why bulldoze it? It was heartbreaking to consider. And even worse, I wasn't sure there was much I could do to prevent it. All I *could* do was clean the place up, bring it back to working order, try to finagle a digital catalogue of some kind, and at least prepare a proposal to show it wasn't going to cost an arm and a leg to maintain the facility.

No one deserved to lose access to books simply because of where they lived.

I was sufficiently warmed up and a little tipsy after my cocoa, busily making notes on my laptop as I deciphered Beatrice's records, when my phone buzzed on the tabletop. It was a text message from a number not in my address book.

Do you like whole wheat?

I stared at the message before snorting. It had to be Miles.

Stalker. How'd you get my number? I texted back, having to wait a minute for it to actually send. I needed to buy a better router.

Mr. Fields.

Employment information not confidential in small towns?

The little writing bubbles popped up, vanished, then popped up and left again.

I sent another message. *I'm kidding.*

Oh. Good.

What's this about wheat bread?

Do you like it? Miles responded.

You know you can call me if you want to chat about bread.

His bubbles popped up again, followed by *I don't like talking on the phone.*

I chuckled. Miles's shyness was actually adorable as hell. The juxtaposition—a tall, strong, blue-collar sort of guy too bashful to have a phone conversation—was interesting. And attractive. Miles Sakasai was definitely the kind of guy I'd like to go on a date with, if he were interested. And I was pretty sure, after spending the day with him, he was at least a little into guys. But was he into *me* specifically?

Maybe. Because I think we were flirting over bread.

I like wheat bread. Do you?

I was going to make some for tomorrow.

Lunch is on me, remember? I texted back.

It's okay.

How about I bring sandwich makings, and you bring bread?

It took a moment for his message to come through, but Miles answered, *I'd like that.*

I didn't hear from him again that night. I assumed he was kneading or punching or doing whatever. I would have enjoyed talking to him for real, what with that gravelly, sexy voice of his, but I stayed busy with a second mug of adult cocoa and my records. I eventually moved to the couch, which was haphazardly situated in the middle of the living room, surrounded by still-unpacked boxes, where I fell asleep with a ledger covering my face.

CHAPTER THREE

"Good morning."

I was crouched in front of the minifridge, shoving some groceries inside for future lunches at the library. I shifted and looked up. Miles was standing over me.

"Hello, Mr. Sakasai," I said with a broad smile. "I didn't think to ask last night what sort of sandwiches you like, so I brought a bunch of choices."

"You're very thoughtful." He set a wrapped loaf of bread down on the counter.

Miles was wearing some old jeans with paint stains and another T-shirt that fit him like a glove. I peered closer at his colorful arms—tattoos of a goldfish, a pirate ship on the sea, and Japanese woodblock art of some cats and a woman in a kimono. It was a very eclectic bunch of art, but all extremely well done. So he must have gotten paid pretty well elsewhere in town.

Miles glanced sideways at me. "My father doesn't approve."

"Of your tattoos?"

"He's a very old-school man."

"What's that mean?"

"When he was growing up in Japan, tattoos still had a stigma. Something the public associated with criminals or gangsters," Miles explained.

"I think they're gorgeous."

"Thank you."

"Did they hurt?" I asked.

Miles shook his head. "No. Well—the one on my inner thigh was a bit uncomfortable."

My mind took that image and ran with it like a bat out of hell. What in the world was tattooed there? How long did the artist have their head in Miles's crotch?

I'd like to be in his crotch....

"You okay?"

My cheeks were hot and my pants felt a bit too tight. "Tease." I walked out of the kitchenette.

I heard Miles chuckle to himself as he followed me out. "Christopher," he said, catching my elbow at the stairs. "May I ask you a question?"

I looked up, cocking my head to the side. "Of course."

"I was thinking, last night… would you… be interested in dinner? With me. *Of course*. At my house," he said, stumbling a bit. God, he was so cute, and nervous and hopefully as excited as I felt.

"I'm surprised," I said.

"That I like men?"

"No. Yes—no, I suspected you might have. I just thought I'd be the one who'd end up asking *you* out in the next few days." I absently tugged on my sweater. "You didn't strike me as the 'ask a guy out' sort."

Miles shifted a bit. "I don't. Not that much."

"I'd really like to have dinner with you," I said.

His mouth quirked into a small smile. "Tonight?"

"Sure. How did you know about me, though?"

"Easy." He moved by and started down the staircase. "You were checking me out yesterday."

"I was not," I protested.

"You were."

"I was just looking at your tattoos."

Miles stopped and turned to stare at me. "You were checking me out," he said again.

I rolled my eyes and huffed. "Fine. I checked you out, and I *liked* what I saw."

I had estimated the cost and time it would take to put the library into a digital catalogue and convert the old glue-a-card system into scanned bar codes. If Beatrice's numbers were right, there were only about six thousand books in the library, so while it'd take considerable time, it was less than what I'd expected. If that could be completed first, before dedicating more budget to new inventory, we'd be ahead of the game. But Lancaster needed more books for sure, so that couldn't be put off too long. The neighboring libraries, according to their websites, had between twelve and thirty thousand books on hand, both in traditional format as well as audio. I had *no* audio. I also had no magazine subscriptions like some libraries did, if you didn't count the *National Geographic* from fifteen years ago up in the storage room.

Going back several years in Beatrice's books showed an average annual budget of less than twelve thousand dollars to maintain the library, not including her meager salary. I supposed, based on utility records and purchases made, the building *could* continue to be maintained on that paltry sum, but to bring our community into the future, I wanted to raise the budget to twenty thousand.

At least.

That didn't include my own income either. And since I was a man who fancied something other than ramen noodles for dinner seven days a week, I wanted more than the criminal salary they'd been offering Beatrice.

Logan Fields had arrived before lunch to see how I was doing, and the numbers I'd proposed were giving him flop sweat. Literally. He wiped his brow and upper lip with a handkerchief. "Twenty thousand is impossible, Christopher."

"I could manage with eighteen," I countered. "But you must understand, this community deserves to have what these bigger towns and cities take for granted."

"Of course I agree with you," Logan replied. "But other Selectmen will make this difficult for me."

"You mean Sam?"

He leaned forward in the chair in front of my desk, the legs creaking under his weight. "I suppose he came and introduced himself."

"Yes. All but told me to fuck off. Pardon my language."

"I'm sure he did," Logan muttered, looking down at his hands with a scowl.

"Mr. Fields, is there any way to get a small sum in advance?"

"Chris—"

"We can put the entire library online," I said, cutting him off. "I know about web design, enough to make a little home page. I mean, we don't even have a sign out front to advertise hours, let alone being searchable on the internet.

We can look into having someone list all of the books on the website so folks can see what's available. We can make a request form to get the community's input on future purchases, to *ensure* foot traffic."

Logan patted his upper lip with the handkerchief again. "What sort of money are we talking about?"

I glanced over Logan's shoulder and watched as Miles exited the disaster room, pulling his bandana down from his mouth. No doubt breathing in the dust was troublesome. "Well, the bar code system would only cost a few hundred." I quickly kept talking, because he looked a bit too hopeful. "The digital inventory software… I found one for a little under two grand."

"Two *grand*?"

"And I can make a cheap website for a few hundred more, but once we get back on our feet, I'd seriously suggest hiring a professional to oversee it."

Logan shook his head, groaning as if he had indigestion.

Miles made eye contact with me as he passed by the checkout desk to go upstairs.

"I know it's a lot, but this will give the state the records and numbers they want, Mr. Fields. *Please*," I finished, consciously having to stop gripping my hands together in desperation.

"I can pay for Mr. Sakasai to fix the shelves," Logan said after a pause. "And I can pay for you. I'm certain I can get you a few hundred for the bar code system, but that's it."

"Mr. Fields—"

"No," he said. "I just can't. I have no budget left. I'm sorry, Christopher, but you've got to find a way to get the state what they need without buying this computer software." He stood and gathered his coat. "I'll get that check cut for you by the weekend. Send me the total cost, will you?"

"Yes, sir," I said quietly, defeat sinking my gut like a stone in water.

Logan said goodbye and saw himself out. I sat at the desk for a while longer. All I needed was three grand and I could do it—could prove we deserved our annual budget, and in fact deserved *more*. I was already so in love with this library that I'd have spent my own savings to pick up the software, but I had *nothing* left after moving here.

The wind outside picked up, howls passed through the trees, and snow whipped up in pretty spirals around the windows.

It felt like Sam Bloom had already won. What was the point in fighting? I dragged myself from the chair, went upstairs, and stopped in the doorway of the kitchenette. Miles was making sandwiches at the counter.

He looked over his shoulder. "It didn't go well," he stated.

I shook my head. "I need three thousand dollars for inventory software, a bar code system, and a website. I only get the bar code system. But that's not enough. The Board wants me to provide real data to prove how much the library is utilized, and I can't do that without all of the tools."

"Come sit." Miles put the sandwiches on the table.

I walked across the room and collapsed in the closest chair. "If I hadn't spent all of my money moving up here, I'd just buy it myself."

Miles sat across from me. "Eat."

"I'm too upset."

"Being upset on an empty stomach will only make it worse."

I sighed, maybe a little dramatically, and picked up the sandwich. Miles had chosen the chicken slices, added some lettuce, tomato, mayonnaise, and with his bread, it was an award-winning combination.

"It's really good," I mumbled.

Miles tore at his crust. "May I ask, why are you so invested?"

I looked up. Miles was staring intently, waiting for an answer. "It's silly, right?"

"No."

"I feel like I've always been looking for a place to belong. And I feel that here. I know it's sudden—I've been working all of two days—but I love Lancaster so far, and I love the history within these walls. And there's nothing sadder than losing books. Don't you think?"

Miles looked thoughtful. "My father went on a lot of business trips, back and forth to Japan. My mother and I were never very close, so I was lonely when he was gone. And... I've always been shy. That hasn't changed much. But I spent a lot of time here when my father was away. The smell of the books is nostalgic—reminds me of summer vacations or cold winter days sitting in the alcoves, reading."

"There must be others who feel like you do, right?"

"Yes."

I took another bite of food. "I won't give up until they fire me, but I feel like the blow I got from Mr. Fields all but confirmed it's a lost cause."

"Don't say that." Miles didn't smile, but he reached out and touched my arm briefly. "I'll do whatever I can to help."

I thanked Miles. He nodded and busied himself with lunch and the morning newspaper he'd brought with him. I ate my own sandwich while trying to read the headlines upside down.

"There's a fair?" I finally asked.

Miles glanced up. "Hmm? Oh. Yes, the annual holiday food fair is this weekend."

"That sounds fun. What sort of things do they have?"

Miles waved a hand. "There's live music, restaurants and businesses in town set up booths to sell food, there's a cooking contest…."

"Are you going?" I asked next.

Miles looked down at the newspaper again. "I was thinking about entering the cooking competition," he said by way of answer, scratching the side of his nose absently. "*Maybe.*"

"Oh my God," I said, feeling much happier with this discussion versus the doom and gloom of the library's sad fate. "Do it! What will you enter?"

Miles shrugged. "Bread."

"Well, duh. I've no doubt you'll win."

He laughed nervously and was definitely blushing. "That's nice of you to say, but I'm not—"

"No, no, don't say some little old lady has a secret blueberry pie recipe that's greater than your orgasmic bread."

"Orgasmic?"

"Your bread satisfies the pleasure principle of the id," I said, grinning as Miles snorted and nearly choked. "Come on! It'll be fun. I'll go with you, if that's okay."

"That sounds nice."

I peeked into the out-of-order room as Miles finished for the day. "Wow, this is major progress."

He stood from shutting his tool kit and picked it up. "The shelves built into the walls are fixed, but these standing shelves need to be reinforced. Some aren't salvageable. I'll build new ones to replace them."

I must have had a look on my face. Even crappy shelves would cost money, and me without a piggy bank to bust open for a rainy day.

Miles said, "Don't worry. I'll deal with the fees and Selectmen."

I nodded.

"Come to dinner?"

"Now?" I looked at my watch.

"I want to teach you to bake bread. It takes a while."

I grinned and crossed my arms over my chest. "Oh, really? Are we going to do it à la Patrick Swayze in *Ghost*? You get close behind me, put your hands over mine, and— *knead dough*?" I asked suggestively.

Miles shook his head as he walked past and left the room. He was singing "Unchained Melody" under his breath. God, I hoped my baking lesson ended with some touchy-feely time at a pottery wheel—sans the pottery wheel.

After Miles helped me close the library for the night, I followed him in my car to a big Queen Anne Victorian home not far from the center of town. Even in the dark, I could make out the bright paint, massive porch, and the ancient trees with branches hanging over the lower roof. I got out of my car, my breath coming out in frozen puffs in the cold night air.

"This is some place," I said.

Miles locked his truck, then motioned for me to follow. I hurried behind, snow crunching loudly under our feet. Inside, his home was an interesting mix of country aesthetic and no doubt expensive antiques that better suited the elegant home. Miles hadn't struck me as an antique-y sort of guy, but then again, he didn't seem to be the sort who baked and sang fifties love songs either.

He took my coat and hung up our winter garments before leading the way into a large kitchen. "Wait here."

I stood at the counter, watching Miles go into the wide-open living room. He turned on the television, brought up an instant movie account, flipped through the options for a moment, then selected one. *Ghost* started playing.

"I knew it," I said as Miles came back and washed his hands at the sink. "You're a big softie, aren't you?"

"A little."

"Patrick Swayze your kind of guy?"

Miles shook his head. "No. You are, though." He dried his hands on a towel. "This whole librarian thing you have going on is cute."

I glanced at myself. Different checkered pants, a tie, baggy gray sweater buttoned up the front—okay, I *definitely* looked the part now. "Cute, huh?"

"Sexy," he corrected.

"Yeah?"

Miles shrugged one shoulder and grabbed two mixing bowls. "Here's your bowl."

"We're really baking bread?"

"Yes." He fetched little packages and set them beside me. "Here's your yeast."

"Yummy."

"You have to be gentle. Yeast is a living thing. You mix it with water, but if it's too cold, it won't grow, and if it's too hot, you'll kill it."

Miles did the finger test with the water, but then confirmed he was right with a thermometer. He expertly stirred his concoction, almost as if it were second nature to him, and instructed me how to do the same with my own. I had thought it was sort of goofy at first—I mean, this was a date, and we were baking bread—but watching Miles in his element was nice. He was so chill and relaxed while cooking, his smile unguarded and easily offered. Even his shoulders seemed to loosen up. Miles might have been good at making repairs, and physical labor clearly paid the bills, but he loved baking more than anything.

"Why bread?" I asked as he took the dough out of the bowl and I did the same with mine. "Of all things?"

"It's both a science and an art," he said. "Measuring your ingredients is straightforward—it has the same results every time. But kneading dough isn't easy. You pull forward and push back and turn just a little before doing it again. If you're too rough, the dough will be heavy or it could end up full of air, neither of which makes for good eating."

"I think that's the most you've ever said in one breath," I replied.

Miles ignored the jab, looked at my dough, then slowly performed the kneading motion on his own. "Like this."

I watched a few times and tried to mimic. "Good?"

"Fold it over more." He again performed the motion.

I did so.

"You're too rough."

"What are, things I never want to hear in bed," I said, trying the kneading motion once more.

That got another little laugh out of Miles. "You're cute."

"So you've said."

"At the cost of another sex joke, you're still too rough," he stated.

I paused and looked up at him. "Oh, come on. You have to stand behind and knead with me. This is a *prime moment*."

"Is it?"

"This will make or break our future together," I joked.

Miles stopped working his dough and stepped behind me. He was warm and solid, and as Miles slid his arms around me and put his hands over my own, it was like finding home.

Miles tilted his head to the side, resting close to mine. "Like this," he murmured as he guided my hands.

"I could get used to this," I replied, falling into the calm repetition of fold, press, turn.

"It's nice," Miles agreed. He planted a kiss on the side of my head.

The night turned out to be one of the sweetest and most enjoyable dates I'd ever been on. No awkward small talk, no trying to find where you clicked with the other person. Miles was so easy to get along with, and by the time the bread was baking, we were drinking wine and laughing as if we'd shared that moment in his kitchen a hundred times before. Unfortunately, I wasn't very good with wine. I remembered eating the bread—Miles's was better than mine, naturally—and pasta afterward, I believe, but the rest of the night....

I vaguely remembered trying to kiss Miles. I mean *kiss* kiss, like let's-get-it-the-fuck-on, and him stopping me. Then nothing. So when I woke up in his bed, I was more than a little confused.

"Good morning."

I grunted and rolled over to see Miles sitting on the edge, holding a cup in one hand. "Why am I here?"

"I wasn't going to let you drive home last night," he replied. "Here. Have some water."

I sat up, took the cup, and downed the drink in one go. "I'm sorry," I said when I came up for air. "I should have only had one drink. Me and red wine don't mix."

"It's okay. You're an adorable, handsy drunk."

"Am I?"

Miles set the cup on the nightstand. "I slept on the couch."

"Oh, Miles, I'm sorry. I didn't—"

He waved a hand. "It's all right. *Really.*"

"You're so chivalrous. What time is it?"

"About six o'clock. I came to see if you wanted breakfast."

Miles had cooked dinner, given up his bed, and now wanted to continue tending to me the next day? This sort of princess treatment was going to go to my head.

"I almost can't handle you," I stated.

"What should I do to make sure that doesn't happen?" he countered.

I rubbed my forehead with one hand.

"Headache?"

"A little," I answered. "Couple of painkillers will do the trick."

"Want a shower?" Miles asked next.

I glanced up. "With you?"

He stared at the bedspread for a moment, shrugged, and said, "Sure."

Wow. That was easy.

Miles stood, offered a hand, and pulled me out of bed. He led me into the adjoining bathroom, shut the door, and turned on the taps to let the water warm up. He took off his pajamas, revealing a tattooed chest and back to match his arms. I loved the choice of such vibrant colors. The bold line work on some of the tattoos was mesmerizing, and I nearly forgot to check for that inner-thigh art Miles had mentioned before.

A bird on a flowering branch. *Very* pretty.

"Did the tattoo artist get a glimpse of your cock?" I whispered.

Miles moved closer and started unbuttoning my shirt. "Yes."

"How'd that work out for you?"

Miles slid the shirt off my shoulders and then worked on the front of my pants. "Well, it was a she, so less exciting for me."

I laughed and stepped out of my clothes. Miles was half-hard, but I had a flagpole that wouldn't quit, hungover or not. And frankly, I couldn't fault my physical response. Miles was gorgeous.

The steam and heat from the shower were nice, but Miles wrapping his arms around me and kissing me was a million times better. He ran his hands down my sides, around my back, and settled them on my ass. He pulled me closer against him. Miles slipped his tongue into my mouth as we kissed. God, he tasted good.

Like coffee and mint toothpaste and man.

Perfect.

Shivers of excitement cascaded down my spine as Miles moved his hands along my body again. He kissed and nipped the side of my neck, running his tongue from my Adam's apple to the hollow of my throat. He tilted his head, bit down where my neck and shoulder met, and began stroking my cock.

"Oh God," I groaned. "Don't stop." I wrapped an arm around Miles's neck, holding him close. I shoved a hand between us and started touching him too.

Miles panted quietly. "A bit tighter," he instructed.

I adjusted my grip on him, giving his cock long strokes and running my thumb over the head.

Miles sped up. The only obvious goal in mind was to make me come until I *maybe* passed out. "You like this?" he asked.

"Yes," I said, moaning unabashedly.

He kissed me hard.

My knees nearly buckled. I said against his lips, "Next time. Sex? Until I can't walk."

Miles nodded briefly. "It's a date." He kissed me again and thrust a finger between my asscheeks.

"*Shit*...." I pressed my forehead against Miles's chest, watched my hand on his dick, and focused on that delicious tease of what "next time" would entail.

I can say with absolute certainty that the best hand job and fingering I'd ever had was from Miles. Kudos to the guy who worked with his hands for a living. Miles was both gentle and thorough, bringing me to the edge faster and more efficiently than any lover I'd had in the past. His hands were rough, and his callused skin made every part of my body feel like both fire and electricity at once.

I'd never screamed from a hand job, but I think his neighbors heard me that morning. And after we finished and washed, he kissed my lips and made pancakes.

CHAPTER FOUR

When it came time for the fair that weekend, I realized it was a far bigger deal than Miles had led me to believe. It was like the entire town came out for it. Maybe neighboring ones too. After much fretting and baking more bread than he really knew what to do with, Miles had settled on a loaf of sourdough for the competition. The judges had taste-tested earlier in the day, and afterward the tent was opened to the public to sample the competing pieces.

Miles was nervous, which was precious. "There are a lot of people in the contest," he said as we surveyed the rows of cakes, pies, stews, and other submissions.

I rubbed his back and he absently put an arm over my shoulder to pull me closer. "True, but look—your bread is gone."

"Is it?"

I pointed to where there was a sign with his name and an empty plate.

"Maybe they tossed it."

"Miles, don't be silly."

"It wasn't my best."

"Yes, it was."

"I can do better."

"I'm sure," I agreed. "But they judged *this* piece. So there's nothing you can do about it."

"I should have done rye bread."

"Sourdough is superior." I looked at him. "Don't worry. It's just for fun. Want to go take a hayride?"

"They announce the winners soon."

"All right. Let's get drunk on hard apple cider."

Miles glanced down. "Maybe a drink wouldn't hurt." He dropped his arm as he turned, and we both nearly collided with Sam Bloom.

Great. The guy who wanted to shove me off a theoretical cliff.

But Sam seemed equally surprised and looked back and forth between us. "Miles," he finally stated.

Miles was really excellent at neutral expressions, and with the naturally gentle way in which he spoke, it was difficult to tell if he was upset or not. Even though he was so nervous about this food competition, I'd have hardly known it from his deep, calm voice. So in fact, the only reason I knew there was an *issue* between him and Sam was because it was Sam's expressions that gave it away. Just like at the library, there was a crackle of energy between them, and not the good kind.

"Hello, Sam," Miles said cordially.

Sam had already made up his mind about me. I was a roadblock he'd easily run over in a few weeks. His personal issue was with Miles. "Can I speak with you for a minute, Miles?"

Miles nodded and touched my arm briefly. "I'll be right back."

I stood just inside the tent, watching them outside. Miles had his hands in his coat pockets, saying nothing as Sam spoke animatedly, pointing this way and that, but more often than not in my direction. A few people glanced at them, but Miles didn't flinch under the curious looks or Sam's growing volume.

When Miles finally did speak, of course I couldn't hear it, but it shut Sam up fast. I might have only lived in this town for a few weeks and had known Miles for a total of *five days*, but I wasn't born yesterday. Sam was an ex who clearly wasn't over a breakup. I felt a little bad, because even though I thoroughly disliked him for wanting to take my job and bulldoze the library, Miles was swoonworthy and I could see how not having him anymore would hurt.

Miles patted Sam's upper arm and walked back toward me. Sam watched him a moment longer, then turned and quickly walked away.

"Cider?" Miles asked, picking up our conversation like nothing had happened.

"Uh… everything all right?"

"We dated for two years. I broke up with Sam three months ago. It wasn't an amicable end."

"Why?"

Miles took my hand and led the way out of the tent and toward the vendor booths. "Someone who loves you shouldn't want to change you. Sam didn't like how I expressed myself."

"Yeah, well, he's nuts."

"Why do you say that?"

Because Miles wasn't the sort of man who needed to *speak* in order to express himself. Like that shower we'd shared—I'd understood so well what he was feeling. His pleasure, joy, contentment. And clearly Sam hadn't spent a lot of time in the kitchen with Miles, because he'd have seen the difference it made when Miles was somewhere that he felt safe and happy.

"I think you do just fine," I said simply.

The fair had taken over the entirety of Main Street, effectively shutting down traffic for the day. Loud music came from an open lot nearby where a band played on an assembled stage. We walked hand in hand down the middle of the road, passing roaming groups of kids, families, and other couples. We stopped at the Snowy Ridge Apple Orchard booth for cider. The line was ridiculously long, but after taking my first sip of the hot beverage, I understood why. It was like spiked liquid gold.

"I really like living here," I said after a moment.

"I'm glad," Miles answered. He let go of my hand and moved to stand in front of me. "Christopher?"

I squinted a bit, looking up at Miles's weirdly serious expression. "Something wrong?"

"Will you be my boyfriend?"

Oh.

"We aren't already?"

Miles's brows knitted together. "No…."

I snorted. "I'm sorry. I don't think I've ever been asked so formally before. I guess I assumed. We're in such good sync together, aren't we?"

His face softened, and Miles let out a held breath. "Yes, very much."

"I would absolutely *love* to be your boyfriend," I replied. I stood on my toes to kiss his mouth. "The deal has been sealed."

"Hey-ho, folks!" A man's voice thundered through the sound system. "Come on over to the stage. We're gonna be announcing the winners of the cooking contest here in just one minute. Come on down, come on!"

"That's your cue," I said, grabbing Miles's hand and hauling him away from the cider booth.

Miles was dragging his feet. "I've changed my mind. I'm not going to win. I'd rather—you said you wanted to do the hayride."

"Nope, not until they announce your name. Pardon me, excuse me," I said, weaving through the growing crowd to get a good place near the stage.

I hadn't tried samples from the other cooks, but I liked to think I wasn't biased in my belief that Miles was phenomenally talented. I wanted to see him win so badly, just so he couldn't deny the recognition.

"Thank you all for entering," the man on stage said as he was handed a sheet of paper. "I know the judges certainly enjoyed the competition." The crowd chuckled. The announcer cleared his throat. "Third place goes to Lucy Black for her blueberry pie."

"Old lady?" I whispered to Miles.

He struggled to keep his amusement under wraps. "Yes."

"*See*? She got third."

"Second place," the man continued, "goes to George Albertson for his beef stew. And, drumroll, please…. The winner of the forty-sixth annual winter cook-off is Miles Sakasai for his sourdough bread. Congratulations!"

Miles looked confused for a beat, almost as if the words failed to sink in. But then a few people surrounding us urged him forward while clapping him on the shoulder. Miles left my side, climbed the steps of the stage, and accepted a blue ribbon and envelope from the announcer.

I cupped my hands around my mouth and shouted, "Go Miles! I *told* you."

"He's a lucky bastard," the woman beside me said.

I glanced at her and couldn't help but ask, "Why's that?"

"The prize money," she replied. "If I could cook to save my life, I'd have entered in a heartbeat."

"There's prize money?" I repeated.

Her companion peered around her and at me. "Hell yeah, there's prize money," he declared. "Five thousand dollars. If I had that, I'd go on vacation. Go to Florida for a few weeks."

"Oh yeah," the woman agreed. "Treat yourself to the snowbird life."

I looked back at the stage. I guess that was why Miles had been so nervous about the results. But he was smiling—a big, bright grin on his face as he made his way back through the crowd.

It melted my heart.

Logan Fields ordered the bar code system as promised. I'd received it a few days after the food fair and was at the library, trying to install the program on my laptop and figure it out. The front door opened and I glanced up from where I sat at the checkout desk.

Miles walked inside. "Good morning, angel."

The *angel* thing had started the other day. I was smitten all over again because of it.

"Howdy." I held up the manual. "I got my bar code system."

"Good," Miles replied. He walked across the room, set his backpack down on the chair in front of the desk, and removed his coat.

"Will you be able to finish the hot mess room today?" I asked, watching as Miles reached into his backpack next.

"Yes. I'll help you carry the books down from storage after."

"Thank you." I raised an eyebrow as he took out an unassuming cardboard box.

"Here you are." Miles thrust it forward.

I pushed up my glasses and took the package. "What is it?"

"Open it."

I smiled and grabbed a pair of scissors from the drawer to cut the tape securing it shut. "What could it be? New Hampshire travel brochures?"

"No."

"A phone book?"

"Just open it."

"I am, I am," I laughed. "I bet it's—Satchel's Digital Inventory?" I held up a manual for the computer software, briefly shuffled through the contents in the box, then looked at Miles hesitantly.

"This is what you needed, right?" Miles asked when I didn't offer an immediate response.

"Y-yes, but, how did you get it?"

"I bought it."

"You *bought* it? Miles. This is two thousand dollars."

"It was the prize money," he said "You're so passionate about saving this library. You care about the well-being of everyday people." Miles shrugged, put his hands on the desktop, and leaned over. "I promised I'd help in any way

I could. Before we met, I was thinking about entering that cooking competition. On the off chance I won, I was going to get some new power tools. But I think this is a better investment."

I felt tears coming on hard and fast, and my vision started getting blurry.

"Please don't cry," Miles hastily added.

I stood, moved around the desk, and nearly knocked Miles down with the hug I gave him. "I'm not," I cried. "You're so perfect. Thank you."

Miles leaned back to kiss my forehead. "Oh." He reached into his pocket and pulled out a folded piece of paper. "And this."

"God, what else did you get me?"

"Estimations on cost and time from a few web designers. I overheard you tell Mr. Fields what you wanted to make, so I emailed some freelancers with your ideas. You can contact them if you want. I'll make the donation to the library to pay for it."

I took the printout and studied the information. "Some of them should be able to get the bare bones up and running before the state's final decision is made."

"Yeah. I said we'd pay to be a priority."

I sniffed again and wiped under my glasses with my free hand. "What if they end up closing this place? You'll have wasted all this money."

"It wasn't wasted," Miles said. "I only got it because I baked some bread."

We spent nearly every day for the next three weeks at the library. Miles, of course, had to work other jobs as they came up once he finished the repairs I'd hired him for, but he always returned to help in his free time. We deep-cleaned the entire building. The wood sparkled and the air was fresh and clean. We organized the back alcove and prepared the side room for use again. We scanned every single title into the inventory, then forwarded that information to our web developer so she could upload it to the site being built. Miles even used the very last of his prize money to buy one desktop computer for community use, which we set up in the study room beside the bay windows.

By the time the Selectmen met with the state about funding, there was nothing more we could possibly do. The library, for what it was worth, was beautiful again. It was catching the attention of residents, and during the final days we had been working to finish before the funding debacle, I opened for customers. Even if it was short-lived, it was gratifying to see so many people come in and out during all hours of the day.

I paced back and forth from the front door to the checkout desk and back again.

Miles was sitting, calm as ever, at the chair in front of the desk. "The floor is already worn out there, angel."

"What?"

"You're going to walk right through it and into the basement."

"I'm nervous."

"I know."

"Why hasn't Mr. Fields called? What's taking so long? Is the heat too high in here?"

"I think it's you," Miles suggested.

I grumbled and loosened my tie. The anticipation was worse than a kid on Christmas morning being told to wait to open presents, combined with the dread that accompanied a dentist's drills just before getting a root canal. I was halfway to crazy, waiting for Mr. Fields to call and tell us the results of his meeting, when he actually showed up at the front door instead.

"Christopher," he called gleefully, face beaming.

"Oh my God," I said, holding my hands up. "Yes? *Yes*?"

"Yes," he declared. "They're keeping the library open!"

I screamed, which of course one should never do in a library, and jumped up and down like a damn kid. I gave him a hug and then embraced Miles as he joined us.

"Now listen," Logan said with a grin. "Twenty thousand was shot down, like I told you, but they agreed to seventeen annually, plus your salary. In two years, they want to review your progress. If significant usage proves a larger budget is needed, it will be taken into consideration then. And now that we have time on our side again, we can pursue grants for additional major purchases."

I couldn't believe it. This was all a dream come true. I had my home, my boyfriend, and my job.

"I'll take that as a major win," I said happily. I shook Logan's hand again. "Thank you for trusting me."

"Thank *you*, Christopher. Otherwise I'd be locking this door for a final time." Logan looked at Miles. "And thank you for your generous donation, Mr. Sakasai. I hear it was all due to your cooking skills?"

"Ah, well… yes," he admitted quietly.

I looked at Miles. "*Books and Bread: A Love Story*."

"Dork."

C.S. Poe is an author of gay mystery, romance, and speculative fiction. She is a winner of the FAPA, Next Generation, and e-Lit book awards, as well as a finalist of the Lambda Literary, Next Generation, and EPIC awards.

She resides in New York City, but has also called Key West and Ibaraki, Japan, home. She loves Romanticism artwork, Gilded Age New York, the films of Buster Keaton, coffee in the morning and whiskey in the evening, true crime, and cats. She's rescued two cats—Milo and Kasper do their best to distract her from work on a daily basis.

C.S. is an alumna of the School of Visual Arts.

Her debut novel, *The Mystery of Nevermore*, was published 2016.

cspoe.com

ALSO BY C.S. POE

SERIES:
Snow & Winter
The Mystery of Nevermore
The Mystery of the Curiosities
The Mystery of the Moving Image
The Mystery of the Bones
The Mystery of the Spirits

Snow & Winter Collection
Interlude

Magic & Steam
The Engineer
The Gangster
The Doctor

A Lancaster Story
Kneading You
Joy
Color of You

The Silver Screen
Lights. Camera. Murder.

Memento Mori
Madison Square Murders
Subway Slayings
Broadway Butchery

An Auden & O'Callaghan Mystery
(co-written with Gregory Ashe)
A Friend in the Dark
A Friend in the Fire

NOVELS:
Southernmost Murder

NOVELLAS:
11:59

SHORT STORIES:
Curio
Love in 24 Frames
That Turtle Story
New Game, Start
Love Has No Expiration

CONNECT WITH C.S. POE

Visit cspoe.com for the latest book and audio releases, as well as available translations.

Join C.S. Poe's newsletter for information on upcoming projects, read advance excerpts and free flash fiction, stay up-to-date on sales, conference appearances, and much more!

Follow C.S. Poe on Goodreads to keep your books organized and reviewed and BookBub to be the first notified of new releases and sales!

Check out C.S. Poe's other social media.

Website:

cspoe.com

Newsletter:

https://www.subscribepage.com/cspoelanding

Goodreads:

https://www.goodreads.com/author/show/13832392.C_S_Poe

BookBub:

https://www.bookbub.com/profile/c-s-poe

Other Social Media links:

https://linktr.ee/cspoe